John Kelly

SOPHISTICATED BOOM BOOM

V

VINTAGE

Published by Vintage 2004

2 4 6 8 10 9 7 5 3 1

First published in Great Britain in 2003 by
Jonathan Cape

Vintage
Random House, 20 Vauxhall Bridge Road,
London SW1V 2SA

Random House Australia (Pty) Limited
20 Alfred Street, Milsons Point, Sydney
New South Wales 2061, Australia

Random House New Zealand Limited
18 Poland Road, Glenfield,
Auckland 10, New Zealand

Random House (Pty) Limited
Endulini, 5A Jubilee Road, Parktown 2193,
South Africa

The Random House Group Limited Reg. No. 954009
www.randomhouse.co.uk

A CIP catalogue record for this book
is available from the British Library

ISBN 0 099 28596 7

Papers used by Random House are natural, recyclable products made from wood grown in sustainable forests. The manufacturing processes conform to the environmental regulations of the country of origin

Printed and bound in Great Britain by
Bookmarque Ltd, Croydon, Surrey

For Evie

'I guess music is something that we can live by. And we cannot live without it because it's in all of us in some way, in some form, in some fashion. Music can soothe the soul as well as relax the mind. It is one language of love, of understanding, of pain, of hurt, of happiness, of need, of want and desire. Every song has a purpose and should be heard within the heart as well as in the mind. Every song has a meaning. Every song is someone's dream.'

Solomon Burke

AUTHOR'S NOTE

Although real places and events are referred to, this is a work of almost total fiction, and particularly unreliable is material written in the first person. All quotations attributed to real musicians, however, are taken from interviews with the author.

My memory of the lyrics of 'By the Shortcut to the Rosses' (Nora Hopper), 'The Sash My Father Wore' and 'The Shan Van Vocht' was refreshed by *Rich and Rare – A Book of Ireland* by Sean McMahon. 'In North America' is sung by Frank Harte on the album *Daybreak and Candle-End* and the words of 'Lough Erne Shore' come from Paddy Tunney and are found in his book *The Stone Fiddle – My Way to Traditional Song*. Thanks also to Gabriel McArdle for 'Lovely Lough Erne's Shore' sung so beautifully down the phone.

Some historical information on Enniskillen was culled from the following sources: *The Fermanagh Story* by Peadar Livingstone; *Enniskillen – Historic Images of an Island Town* by Helen Lanigan Wood; and *Ordnance Survey Memoirs of Ireland – Parishes of Co. Fermanagh* edited by Angelique Day and Patrick McWilliams. Vital details of Celtic mythology were checked with *Over Nine Waves* by Marie Heaney.

Thanks are due to many friends and colleagues for sharing their time, energies, expertise and gifts. To my editor at Jonathan Cape, Robin Robertson. To Patsey Murphy, Gerry Smyth and Deirdre Falvey at the *Irish Times*. To Paul Brady, David Hammond, Elvis Costello, Séamas MacAnnaidh and Gavin Friday. To Hank Norwood of Belfast for a truly unique musical education. To Tom Dillon in New York. To Tommy and Lily Kelly. To Catherine and Evie. And to the thousands of musicians, dead or alive, who continue to lift the heart and ease all paths.

'Sophisticated Boom Boom' is a song by the Shangri-Las.

PRETTY VACANT

'I went along to see the 101'ers and supporting them was the Pistols. And that's when I saw God. I saw this little red-haired Paddy – up there, pouring beer over his head and sneering at the audience who were shouting insults at him. And then he'd launch into this loud, raucous rock 'n' rollin' number with foul lyrics. I thought this was the pop band I'd been waiting for all my life.'

Shane MacGowan

A sweaty dive in 1977. The Sex Pistols, rigid with noise and ferocity, are hacking through a high-speed 'Pretty Vacant' and Johnny Rotten, his eyes ablaze, is staring me right in the face.

Lydon! I mouth up at him. My name is Lydon! Same as yours! Me name is the exact same as yours! Lydon fuckye! Lydon!

He can't hear you, ye big bollocks! Spit Maguire shouts in my ear, the force of his wet voice hurting like a punch, as if Johnny Rotten gives two shites what your name is!

I dunt Spit away and try again to make direct contact with the arch-punk, but he just swivels and glares with a chilling straitjacket venom at the balcony, the bastard deliberately ignoring me now as I keep pointing viciously to my chest.

My name is Deccy Lydon! Ly-don! Ly-don! My name is Deccy Lydon! Deccy Lydon!

But Johnny Rotten just clings harder to his microphone stand and twists his neck like a lizard – goading me with a spiteful look of feigned terror and contempt. He cannot hear me. He doesn't want to hear me. Spit is right as usual. He doesn't give a damn that I am Deccy Lydon. And why should he give a damn? The mad bastard doesn't give a damn about anything.

He's some fuckin' tulip! laughs Spit into my face, his breath stinking of Embassy Regal and Juicy Fruit. He's a fuckin' loo-la! Like all the loo-la Lydons!

And then as the feedback begins to squeal and Rotten unkinks his neck once more, I lose it completely – all those years of confused frustrations suddenly rolling into one huge lobbing spit which goes *thup!* and soars like an arcing diamond through the air and lands like stringy glue on the zips of his tartan keks.

You got him! roars Spit. You're fuckin' deadly!

Johnny Rotten, still singing, looks down at his leg and then locks his eyes on me once more and starts screaming at me to fuck off. It is a terrifying moment of connection – scary like all sudden contact and I crumple in shock and panic – just me and Johnny Rotten for three intimate seconds of adrenalin and fear. And just at the point where I think he is about to launch himself at me like a wild fanged cat, Spit Maguire suddenly bounces up on his toes and fires off another spit with the full force of his neck and shoulders.

It is a powerful header on goal and another direct hit – an achievement which causes Spit's entire body to go into a celebratory warp spasm, his teeth jutting jagged in his bottom jaw, his veined eyes bulging and his sugary hair electrifying as his body tightens in convulsions of joyous rage.

Fuck off, yourself! screams Spit up at Johnny Rotten. You're not at home now, you punk bastard!

And so, delighted with ourselves, we punch the air and shudder with the fresh violence of it all. I feel the sinews in my neck about to burst through my skin, and I see myself all nostrils and gums as 'Anarchy in the UK' emerges like a circular saw out of walls of pure white noise. And then, as the whole place begins to bounce and pound, I follow Spit high up into the fizzing air – into the flashes and beams and the chemical smoke – pogo, pogo, pogo – pogo so high that I erupt straight into the lighting rig with a dull crack and a crunch. And all I hear is someone swear in horror and disgust, Oh Jesus!

My scalp splits, a thick sickness rises in my throat and, as I stagger back to earth, a pool of fearful space clears around me. Quickly the blood begins to stream warm through my own sugary punk hair and I start to slip away into a blurred and spinning place. I see only the runny swill of the vodka and blackcurrant and I panic towards puke.

Deccy! You fuckin' mad hoor ye! screams Spit

falsetto, Yaaaaooohhh! You've busted your head, you big tube!

Dazed and dizzy, I'm in trouble and shock. I taste the beery, fag-butt floor and then the blood which runs along the hollows of my face and into my open mouth. I smell the Doctor Martens and the gutties that gather around me, I inhale the soupy cigarette smoke on my own furry jumper and I wish for a frantic moment that I was at home in bed. But still I hear the Pistols cranking it out – fuzzbox, bass and thunderous drums rumbling into me from the cold earth itself.

You're alright, Deccy! Spit laughs in my ear. Are you alright? You're alright! Are you alright? Ah, you're rightly! Only a wee knock!

But it must have been some freewheeling pride which stopped me from passing out completely – some teenage vanity perhaps that kept me conscious enough to see the sheer glory of it all. With one side of my face now covered in my own gore, my punk credentials were assured. Like Shane MacGowan with his ear bitten half-off at the Clash gig, I was now a confirmed and blooded punk, an actual disgrace to St Gavin's School for Boys and a walking work of art. Even Spit himself couldn't top this one and I'd be the talk of the town. And so, lying there bloodstained and sick, I smiled up at Spit with a pride that was real and then laughed aloud in the grave face of eleven stitches and purple puke.

Later that night, as we walked down Mill Street, up Factory Row and home through the dim

Lucozade lights of Enniskillen, via casualty at the Erne Hospital, I delicately fingered the rail track of thread in the crown of my head — my hair now caked in a solid mixture of sugar, blood and some ointment that smelled like the changing rooms in the sports complex. It was quite a wound and I wanted everyone to see it. I had not been this proud since the day I had heroically trailed home a fifteen-pound pike on a forked and bloody branch.

Spit lit a cigarette and offered me one. I knew it would make me sick, so I just took a drag of his, the glowing ash concealed in my palm for a more mean and serious pose — like those grave men at street corners or those hard-boiled seniors who conspired behind the handball alleys and put bets on horses at Newmarket and Chepstow.

I passed the fag back to Spit and he slid it between his lips just to keep it hanging there and look like Keith Richards. And so we walked on, Spit's eyes tortured by his own smoke but still able to speak, cough and cackle all at once. Only for spitting or for making a very severe point indeed would that fag ever be removed. And in our current contented state, Spit was happy to let it dangle the whole way home.

We were in no hurry that night. It was already so late by now that we'd have to sneak in anyway. Another hour or two would make no difference at this stage — the harm was already done. We knew that our parents were already up the walls, searching the place for us, fearing the worst for us, kneeling to pray for us, about to call the police for us, planning to kill us and ready to swing for us – two young punk rockers who went to see the Pistols and crossed time's border into places beyond all sanction and control.

And so we strolled home so careless and easy, both condemned and released, saying little but to rehash the key moments of what we had just witnessed – the night the Pistols had come to Enniskillen and Deccy Lydon and Spit Maguire had been the truest punks of all.

He's fuckin' class, gushed Spit. Johnny Rotten. He's fuckin' class!

Fantastic, I agreed solemnly, I thought he was going to strangle me! You know, when I hit him on the leg, I thought . . .

Did you see the way he stood with his legs like this and him going *Ayeee yam an anar-chist!*?

Fuckin' brilliant! *Ayeee yam an anar-chist!*

What is an *anarchist* anyway?

Don't know. Some class of mad bastard anyway.

And then we smiled and fell quiet again, dragging our feet as we wandered back to our dark one-eye-on-the-clock houses, unwilling and unable to end the night in 1977 that had changed for ever our tiny little lives.

STRICTLY ROOTS

'John was a devout Irishman.'

Yoko Ono

To come at my home town crooked, we might begin many thousands of years ago when the mythological cycle first began to freewheel out of the mist and the Tuatha Dé Danann arrived from across the seas. Crunching the keels of their mighty fleet on to the white beaches of Ireland, they immediately claimed it as their own and, as a certain sign of their intention to remain for ever, they set fire to their ships right there on the strand.

And so, with their boats ablaze and the muscles of King Nuada's jaw twitching, the invaders stood and watched as their past was consumed in a sudden whoosh of flame that rose high into the darkening sky. It was a ship-torching and muscle-twitching which continued for many days and many nights, and it is said that the whole country was filled with a thick, black smoke. Soon the Fir Bolg could only watch in horror as from within these terrible clouds, the Tuatha Dé Danann began to march out steadily into the new, wet land of Ireland.

The slaughter was quick and brutal as Nuada carved his way through the armies of the Fir Bolg,

7

cutting them down in their thousands and driving the few desperate survivors to desolate Atlantic islands and the grim outskirts of Belfast. The old rule of the Bolg was suddenly over and the time of the Tuatha Dé Danann had arrived.

There was, however, a much more daunting and ferocious enemy for Nuada still to overcome. These were the Formorians – a terrible and monstrous people who raided and plundered and kept their neighbours in a constant state of misery and terror. Their demon king – a wild and ugly brute called Balor of the Evil Eye – lived in a gleaming glass tower on Tory Island off the coast of Donegal, and his was a deep, dark and unmusical tale.

Once, when Balor was a young demon, he stopped at the side of the road to listen to chanting coming from a wreck of a house. Looking in the window, he saw several Druids gathered together about their evil work and he was fascinated. But as he peered wide-eyed into that room full of vapours and fumes, the evil gases blew up into his face, blinding him and causing him to let out a cry that was heard all across Ireland. When the Druids discovered him outside, wailing like a cat, they were much alarmed.

We were concocting a most deadly spell, they said. And now the power of that spell has brought death to your eye. From now on, anyone you even glance at will drop dead like a stone! Now fuck away off home! And, whatever you do, keep that eye shut!

And so it was that Balor became known as Balor

of the Evil Eye – feared across Ireland as the dreadful pirate king who destroyed everything he saw. But soon, because he kept his eye so firmly closed at home, he began to lose the power of his eyelid and eventually he couldn't open it at all – the lid just hanging there, heavy and limp, on his terrible face. To open it in battle, however, he had to hire an engineer from Ventry who devised a pulley system with an ivory ring through the flesh of the upper lid and a thick rope which could then be hauled by ten terrified (doomed) Formorians.

Balor's Evil Eye was an irresistible weapon, and soon the brute king had Ireland by the throat, defeating even the magical Tuatha Dé Danann, making them his slaves and plunging Ireland into a reign of terror which might have lasted as far as the Showband Era had it not been for the great Battle of Moytura.

It was here that Balor was eventually toppled – dying, as had been foretold, at the hand of his own grandson (a warrior called Lugh who finally put his awful eye out with a lethal slingshot). And as the Formorians scattered in defeat, the King's wife, Ceithleann of the Crooked Teeth, made good her own escape by diving into Lough Erne and swimming northwards like a wounded serpent. And this is where I come in.

After many days and nights in the freezing water, Ceithleann finally waded out through rushes and glár and crawled on to a small, damp and shady island. And there, halfway between the Upper and Lower

Lough, the broken Queen lay back against a tree and died – her open mouth, her crooked teeth and the foul breath of her causing the very birds to fall dead like chestnuts from the trees. That island then became known as Inis Ceithleann – the Island of Ceithleann – Enniskillen. My home town. The place where I, Declan Patrick Lydon, every day in life, looked out the cracked upstairs window of number 24 The Long Road.

CONFESSIO

'It comes with the time. If I had been fifteen in 1963 I'd
have ended up in a beat group. At another time I might
have ended up in a disco band or a glam band. It just so
happened that the kind of music I started playing was
very rootsy rock 'n' roll. But it was an affectation really.'

Elvis Costello

The truth of course is that we were never punks.
The Pistols never came to Enniskillen and I wouldn't
have gone even if they had. I barely knew who they
were and, in any case, I wouldn't have been let.
Back in 1977, I was still a spotless choirboy and far
too young to be out gallivanting in places where you
could get Embassy Regal, vodka and black, and
lockjaw snogs with local rides and bicycles.

Sid Vicious missed the Summer of Love because
he was playing with his Action Man and my excuse
for missing the Pistols is that I was busy singing songs
about fairies in the school choir. Certainly these
songs were often of beautiful female fairies who
could entrance, beguile and ensnare, but it was all
way over my head in 1977. There's little doubt that
the fairy I met by the short cut to the Rosses was a
potential tutor in the delights of incredible sex, but I

can't say I noticed, and the lush opportunity was
ignorantly missed.

By the shortcut through the Rosses,
    A fairy girl I met;
I was taken by her beauty
    Just like fishes in the net.
The fern uncurled to look at her
    So very fair was she,
With her hair as bright as seaweed
    That floats upon the sea.

By the shortcut to the Rosses,
    'Twas on the first of May,
I heard the fairies piping,
    And they piped my heart away;
And they piped 'til I was mad with joy,
    But when I was alone,
I found my heart was piped away —
    And in my breast, a stone.

By the shortcut to the Rosses
    'Tis I'll go never more,
Lest she should steal also my soul,
    Who stole my heart before.
Lest she should take my soul and crush it,
    Like a dead leaf in her hand,
For the shortcut to the Rosses
    Is the way to fairyland.

But she was wasted on me and so was punk. I was a dull innocent still lost in some pre-pubescent Fermanagh fog — a thick stew from which I could see nothing and appreciate less. Yes, something like punk was impossible to miss, but in our isolated hinterland we missed it completely. I missed it. Spit missed it. We all missed it. And whatever revolution was supposed to be taking place out there on the streets, it certainly wasn't happening anywhere near me — The Long Road, Hillview, Kilmacormick No. 1, Kilmacormick No. 2, Derrygore Terrace, Braeside Park, Loughview Road, Derrin Park, Derrin Road, Riverside, the Cornagrade Road, Queen's Street, Darling Street, Church Street, The Diamond, Townhall Street, East Bridge Street, Belmore Street, Mill Street, Factory Road or Rooney's Path. No sightings there of the Pistols or Joe Strummer or Gaye Advert or Siouxsie or Poly Styrene. No sign there of the air turning blue.

And then when a few sulky punks finally did appear on The Diamond, we were neither shocked nor threatened. In fact, we didn't even know what they were, and simply took them for yet more blow-ins with odd notions, and we sneered grimly at their jaggy hairdos, their dog collars, their purple boots, their bumblebee jumpers and their drainpipes of zippy PVC. Spit, in particular, really took against them and would spend most afternoons after school spitting at them from the upstairs window of the Erne Basin Café.

They're some fuckin' tulips, a disconcerted Spit

would say over his shoulder as he wiped a drooly
one from his chin. See them punks? I fuckin' hate
them.

Are they in a band or something? I would ask.

Aye, and they're shite, so they are.

Are they Hot Vomit? I would ask.

Naw, Hot Vomit's somebody else.

Have you ever seen them? I would ask, more than
curious.

Who?

Hot Vomit.

Naw, but they're shite too.

Are they shite or just shit? I would ask, looking for
clarification.

Naw, they're shite.

And then Spit would resume his purposeful
spitting.

G'won, ya wankers! Fuck off!

This was the way we reacted to most things.
Enniskillen in 1977 was more than just a triangular
island town on the edge of Northern Ireland – it was
also a state of mind which left us entirely remote
from the actual workings of the world. It was like we
were living in some parallel galaxy on which the rest
of the universe had only minor gravitational pulls.
No matter what was going on anywhere else, it
made no difference in Skintown.

Punk, pasta, jogging, herbs, shellfish, cheese, yoga,
vegetarianism, Buddhism, keep-fit, DIY, sex, modern art and wine were typical of a long list of fads and
catchpennies considered ridiculous and unnecessary.

In fact, anything remotely exotic was to be avoided and condemned. A phenomenon involving safety pins never stood a chance.

And so we were the most out-of-touch teenagers on earth and we didn't even know it. When we watched those smart-alecky programmes made specifically for young people by the local BBC we just sat back and snarled. Who exactly were all these whiny teenagers – talking about being bored and wanting to express themselves though drama and modern dance? What was all that about? Who were all these gobshites, banging on about street fashion and 'youth issues'. None of it, not one word of it, made any sense to us and we reacted as normal.

Look at yon wanker! we'd shout at our alien televisions, him and his dyed hair! Must be a fruit!

And even if we had been *real* teenagers with *real* teenage concerns, we'd have got no sympathy anyway. *What have yis got to complain about anyway? Haven't yis got a sports complex? There's nothing only sports complexes. And such oul' nonsense about being bored. And sure how would yis be bored? Nobody was bored in our day. And we didn't have sports complexes coming out of our ears. And now it's all relationships, no less. Relationship this and relationship that. Load of oul' nonsense. There were no relationships when we were your age. You just were glad of an ice cream if you had the price of it. If you were lucky. And you'd be quare and thankful.*

And so we just existed on and on, listening to all this shite while coming up with similarly stupid shite of our own. Not long into our teens we were already cranky old men trapped in our skinny young bodies – always giving out, always slagging off, always condemning everything that made the slightest effort to kick us in our ignorant arses. We were grumpy, old-fashioned, conservative, misinformed, isolated, controlled, fearful, naive, disconnected and as innocent as sin. Meanwhile, all around us, the punk revolution of 1977 raged on regardless. Elvis died. I warbled. Spit spat.

Ten years later a bomb would go off in Belmore Street and the word 'Enniskillen' would come to mean atrocity. They would say 'before Enniskillen' and 'after Enniskillen' and very important people with ashen faces would parachute in to shake hands and speak.

Meanwhile, the town would grieve in dignity and disbelief. Bitterness would take some but most would be uplifted and renewed by a man called Gordon Wilson – a local draper who would talk plainly of forgiveness and love – his lost daughter's hand still warm in his.

BALL OF CONFUSION

'The audience does tend to endow the artist with the content of his own lyric. Sometimes it's important for them that the two are inseparable. I do understand that, and I'm not too bothered because I tend to believe that once the artist has created his work, it's up to the audience to finish it off. I'm absolutely wide open to interpretation.'

David Bowie

Nineteen seventy-nine. Two years after we hadn't seen the Pistols and Spit Maguire was still my pal.

This place is a fuckin' hole! he snapped. It's a bigger fuckin' hole than the Grand fuckin' Canyon! It's like something out of Samuel fuckin' Beckett! I fuckin' hate it!

There was nothing Spit couldn't do with the F-word but his real forte was saliva: torpedoes through his tunnel tongue, snake venom sprayed through his two front teeth, even long-range missiles flicked off the tips of his fingers.

In short, Spit Maguire was the best spitter in the country – a brilliant, fantastic, fabulous genius of the spitting seventies. He had been born for punk, which makes it all the more tragic that he missed it. All that amphetamine sulphate, saliva and rage had surely been his wayward destiny.

I can knock a cleg clean out of the sky, he once bragged, mind the time I hit the fish?

And there is little doubt that if spitting had held any potential for glory, then Spit Maguire would have been the most famous man in Fermanagh. Certainly, if he had lived in the eighteenth or nineteenth century they would have written come-all-ye's about him. In fact, even in 1977, if he had lived in some outlying townland they might still have written come-all-ye's about him. Such heroic material still appeared regularly in the local paper, although they would not publish the one I wrote during double maths, hoping to see it printed the week of Spit's birthday.

Come all ye gallant spitting men and listen to my song
It's only forty verses and I won't detain you long
It's about a gallant hero of honour and renown
He spat and died for Ireland in Enniskillen town.
(And so on.)

But Spit's prowess was already the talk of the whole place. On long summer evenings, crowds would gather to watch him stand like Spartacus in the middle of Darling Street as hundreds of swifts hurtled past him like harpoons, flying low and turning sharply in mid-flight. And people would gasp as Spit picked off the whizzing birds one by one as they dived and whooshed from all directions. It was a spectacle like no other and spectators were often three-deep on the footpath. They even ran buses from out the country.

What are yous all lookin' at for fuck's sake? Spit would mutter under his breath, but I always knew that he was secretly enjoying the whole thing. It lasted for a few glorious weeks, but then the RUC put a heavy-handed stop to it, and then, heavier again, the headmaster of St Gavin's landed out at the Maguires' house for a serious discussion about 'several matters'.

Spit's real name was Ignatius Mary Maguire, but by the time he was nine years old even his parents had come to address him as Spit – a trade name he then insisted on with sulky determination. I once chanced addressing him as Iggy but he took it very badly indeed and huffed with me for six months – spent his time standing on the Cornagrade Road spitting at the lorries.

For most of our young lives, however, myself and Spit Maguire were the bestest of best friends. We were inseparable, and of one confused mind about most things, passing many long hours wondering about what life seemed to be doing to us in our slate-grey northern town.

Certainly we played football and skimmed stones across the lough (on one occasion we skimmed an entire collection of singles belonging to Spit's sister), but most of our time in 1979 was spent just beginning to try to work things out – crouching under lamp-posts, surrounded by our circles of spit, and making what we could of growing up in a place where nothing ever happened.

Bart Maguire (no relation) once suggested that our spitting rituals had been unconscious attempts at necromantic constraint – the pair of us within our circles of moonlit saliva, conjuring angels in the Elizabethan night. We thought this was far-fetched, but when he showed us a picture of Kelley and Dee at their mystical work, we became just a little alarmed about what we might have been innocently engaged in. After all, we knew that we knew nothing much about anything and so there was always every chance of doing something entirely by mistake.

But later we agreed between the two of us that the whole thing had probably been some kind of pavement art – the Jackson Pollock effect revelling both in itself and in chance. But then again, if it was in fact our own spectacular artwork, it was totally unconscious even so. We had never heard of Jackson Pollock – and even if we had, we would have dismissed him as a ballocks beyond belief. That said, our own version of drip and splash surely said something about the way we were barely existing in that timeless, mizzling void?

If it's anything, offered Spit one night, it's Beckett.

Yes, probably, I bluffed.

We had never read any Beckett (or seen anything by him) but Spit had somehow got the gist of *Waiting for Godot* and liked the sound of it. He also liked the sound of Beckett himself because he

seemed to be someone almost as bored as we were –
although our own outlook on life was obviously
bleaker than his.

And so Spit told me all he knew about Samuel
Beckett and soon just the thought of his lonely, grey
existence made some strange sense of our own
soundless exchanges on those clear, frosty nights. In
fact, the mere presence of this apparently grim man
gave us an incomprehensible solace. We consoled
ourselves with the simple thought that if a smart man
like him could sit in silence under a lamp-post, then
so could we.

Crucially, Beckett knew Enniskillen and so he
understood what we were going through. He had
attended Portora Royal School – a building of three
storeys on a basement that stood high on a hill across
the lough from Cornagrade – the Field of the Bones.
And every morning, before his cricket and his
Greek, Samuel Beckett would go for a swim, up as
far as the old castle and back, and boatmen out
spinning with spoons would raise their flat caps and
sigh. They knew full well the danger in which this
bony young man was placing himself because this
was a particularly freezing and pike-infested stretch
of the Erne. But they said nothing. It wasn't their
place to pass remarks. Some kind of Dublin Protestant, they would think to themselves, they don't
know what to be at. Swimming no less. I ask you . . .

But the truth is that no local had ever even
attempted that swim before and it was not until
'Tarzan' Maguire – a great-uncle on my mother's

side – tried it back in 1943 that Beckett's record was threatened. The playwright need not have worried, however, because although Tarzan waded confidently into the glár at the Cornagrade shore and struck out powerfully enough, he went under about a hundred yards from the old castle and was never seen again. To this day, nobody knows whether he was drowned or simply eaten by the fish.

Ah, but Sam, explained Spit, was a wiry hoor. I seen pictures of him and he looks like the Hanging fuckin' Rock. Even when he was a chile he looked like a quarry.

Ah, he's a quare boy alright, I would say, knowing nothing whatsoever about the man we were talking about.

Oh aye, added Spit with pride in his voice, a hardy boy.

To us, Portora Royal School always seemed distant, posh and Protestant, but we were quick enough to take vicarious pride in its famous sons even so. And there were two that we knew of – the first was the Hanging Rock and the second was the curious figure of yet another Dublin Protestant who didn't know what to be at: Oscar Wilde.

We would often speculate about him and what our cornerboy ancestors must have made of him as he strolled along The Brook in his boater, his head in the air and his silk stockings stuck with sticky mickey. And we could only imagine the silent conspiratorial jeers of the townies, unaccustomed to such swank and display.

Would you look at yon sketch . . .

He'd be lost without his daffodils . . .

Aye, true enough . . . daffodils no less . . .

Aw now . . . some class of a Dublin Protestant by the look of him . . .

They don't know what to be at . . .

Wilde seems never to have referred to any of these locals in stories or plays, although there is a locally held suspicion that the character of the Swallow in *The Happy Prince* was based on 'The Swallow' Maguire – a mad, drunken schoolmaster who once claimed he was 'off to Egypt for the Christmas'. Sadly, this particularly dilapidated Maguire never staggered much beyond the East Bridge, but even so, the story stuck. He was supposed to be related to me on my father's side but, typically, was never once mentioned in the house.

But while Portora had Beckett and Wilde, our Alma Mater, St Gavin's School for Boys had damn all. The closest it ever got to Beckett was the wilfully mute Father Grafton who never, ever spoke and once kept his eyes tight shut for a whole year, communicating with his classes by way of scribbles on mimeographed sheets.

The closest it ever got to Oscar Wilde was the time Pius 'The Daffodil' Mullan stood up during one of Grafton's silent classes, declared himself 'a prize fruit' and ran out of the room in tears.

The next day Pius was summarily expelled half-way through an under-16 match against Irvinestown. According to the headmaster, Pius 'The Fruit'

Mullan, as he had since been redesignated, had failed to go in hard for a fifty-fifty ball. Simply intolerable, the headmaster told assembly. This is a *fupboll* school – not amateur dramatics or Gilbert O'Sullivan [sic] or fancy-Dan English literature. This is a *fupboll* school and if there is a fifty-fifty ball there is only one thing for it. You get stuck in! Do you hear me, boys! You get stuck in! You make every tackle a funeral! And yesterday a boy did not go in hard and this is simply intolerable. So ask yourselves the question, boys. And if you're telling me that you are not prepared to go in hard for a fifty-fifty ball then you have no place at St Gavin's because this is a what?

A *fupboll* school, we mumbled.

That's right, boys, a *fupboll* school. In the name of the Father and of . . .

Later that afternoon, back at the scene of the original outburst, Grafton, his eyes shut, circulated a fragrant mimeographed sheet demanding to know the name of the boy who had caused the disturbance the day before. Nobody said anything in reply and so yet another silent double period was spent sneaking in and out for smokes and prodding the slumbering Grafton with a T-square.

So St Gavin's really had bugger all to blow about. It couldn't boast anybody famous at all apart from a priest out in Borneo and the Children of Prague – the notorious performance art band formed by Shay Love after the demise of Hot Vomit. They had released a single called 'There's a Banshee in My Brain' and both Dave Fanning and John Peel had played it, although Peel only played it once and nobody actually heard the programme.

> There's a Banshee in my brain
> There's a dead thing in the drain.
> There's a Banshee, there's a Banshee,
> There's a Banshee in my brain.

But although the Children were without doubt the school's biggest celebrities, St Gavin's was never sure about them, and after the notorious *Bare Arse Tour* of 1980 their tiny picture was angrily removed from the school's entrance hall and a ten-foot papier-mâché hen, which had been constructed by Shay Love in his final year, was violently destroyed by the dean using a fag butt and a can of Three-in-One. When news of the incident spilled down into Enniskillen, Shay was delighted with himself.

'The same way that Portora once erased the name of Oscar Wilde from its scroll of honour,' he told the *Fermanagh Flyer* (his own news-sheet), 'and then, years later, had to write it back with fresh gold paint, the Children of Prague will also have its sweet revenge, not just on St Gav's but also on that fascist, incendiary cleric who burned my gorgeous chicken which took me three months to make. And as for The Bare Arse Tour of 1980, they don't know the half of it.'

25

FUTURE HEN

'They felt freedom in the music. They felt it was
something they could call their own. And they were
damn sure their parents weren't going to like it. Now
that's a fact.'

Sam Phillips

Stravinsky died in 1971, but just like punk, pizza and
pasta, it made no odds in Fermanagh. Nobody
noticed, nobody passed the slightest bit of remarks
and no wake was ever held to discuss the worth of
his life and work. Presumably nobody knew that he
was the man who said that music was the only
domain in which man realised the present. It was a
comment, had we heard it, which would have
explained everything.

Of course, we had no meaningful music at that
time and so we never actually realised the present at
all. In fact, for Spit Maguire and me, nothing ever
really happened in the actual, living moment. What
made it worse was that we couldn't even conjure the
illusion of a here and now because we didn't have a
stereo between us. And a stereo was the only way to
do it. Not that it mattered very much anyway – the
present being a rather undervalued state of affairs
where we lived.

Only the future seemed to ever exist – only a slight possibility of it, certainly – but it was *possibly* there. In fact, in that limited philosophical space in which we grew up, things were constantly being laid out in front of us, like unconvincing carrots. Life, it was constantly implied, would arrive eventually, depending on everything from God to homework – but it was out there somewhere and we might perhaps be rewarded by it when we were much, much older.

Punk, and the reason we'd have loved it if we'd known about it, was about precisely the opposite. It was a fearless declaration that there was no future at all; that there was nothing out there whatsoever but more of the miserable same. And that indicates just how grim we were, that's why Spit liked the sound of Beckett, that's why we were pals, that's why we only laughed at the strangest things and, ultimately, that's the reason we stuck so determinedly with so much that bored us to death.

To think like an actual punk, however, you had to be really conscious of the present and we, quite simply, were not. It was a tense in which only Shay Love existed and that was because he was the singer with Hot Vomit and the Children of Prague and he had seen the Ramones – or at least he said he had seen them. It was the sort of CV which made him unique in the town, if not something of an actual celebrity.

The rest of us were only ever present in the present when we were holding our hands out to be strapped. And even then we were actually slightly in the future as we anticipated the coming pain. Teachers doing the usual ritual punishment thing – leather straps with pet names the way men have stupid names for their penises.

But even the pain of the strap, when it finally arrived, was rarely of the moment either, as we immediately exchanged one hand for the other and anticipated the next blow. Such dull punishments, marking time in the nothingness, made philosophers (and spitters) of us all.

It also explains why Spit Maguire came to elevate spitting to such a high level of artistry. Yes, he made it look easy but he wasn't the best spitter in the country for nothing. Never forget that he spent many dark and desolate hours at it – under those lamp-posts – spitting, thinking and waiting for the silent end of day. And I would be there too. Keeping him company, spitting a bit now and again and thinking about all those things I didn't even know existed. It was a strange, murky, indefinable time and our wise pal Bart Maguire was fit to sum it up the very first day he drifted into our orbit.

There's no future, he said, for a future hen.

He always said things like that. A future hen, he explained to a grim religion teacher with a strap called Tiny Tim, was both the chicken and the egg. Both the egg and the chicken. The teacher just looked up at the light bulb and sighed, *Really*, Mr Maguire?

Bart elaborated. For both chicken and egg, for

both the egg and the chicken, there can never be a future and therefore the long-running argument as to which came first (the future hen or the future hen) was a pointless one.

You *don't* say, Mr Maguire . . .

Oh yes, Father, in fact you'd be a variety of future hen yourself. And so the grim teacher beat Bart Maguire on the wrists with Tiny Tim and then sent him off to the headmaster for more. But the headmaster's weapon of choice (Roger) was fortunately missing and Bart was spared the deliberate pain.

Maybe he's away down to the mart to buy a leather jacket or something? suggested Bart. That's a good one, Father, isn't it? A leather jacket? A leather strap? If you understand me?

The sullen headmaster just groaned and quickly presented Bart with a manky lemon in a brown paper bag and ordered him out, advising him to take the rest of the day off.

If I see Roger, persisted Bart, I'll tell him you were looking for him. If you ask me, there's something going on between him and Tiny Tim. We are all living, loving angels in a world of future hens . . .

Get out, Maguire!

And Bart smiled to himself in the personal knowledge that a week earlier Roger had been kidnapped and was now languishing alone at the bottom of Noon's Hole – a bottomless pit out near Derrygonnelly. He was seeing a girl out there every other weekend – a difficult enough process involving an unreliable bicycle but worth it even so for such easy access to Noon's Hole.

And then there was always Shay Love. We could always depend on him as our genuine rare bird who in his post-Hot Vomit days was really developing as an accidental performance artist. The study hall was his theatre and showtime was any time. One wet Thursday, after ostentatiously eating a large earthworm, he too was dispatched for censure to the headmaster by a nervous substitute teacher too scared to deal with him herself.

Challenged by the weary principal, Shay claimed that what he was doing was 'shock art', the purpose of which was to cause psychological turbulence to this already fragile substitute teacher. It had been a successful exercise too, he said, and added that he saw no need to defend himself because he was a Dadaist. The only one in Fermanagh as a matter of fact.

Well, there'll be no Dada in this school, said the headmaster, we have enough trouble with the chess club. So we'll have no more of your Dada or your funky punky such and such. It's just silly really and very immature. And shave off that beard while you're at it. You're giving a bad example to the first-years.

But they can't grow beards, Father.

Shave it off, Love!

Don't call me love!

And then because the headmaster had rearmed,

Roger having been replaced by Lazarus, Shay returned to class with stinging fingertips and a Johnny Rotten grin. He had clearly endured about six of the best but he walked right over to the trembling substitute teacher, put one reddened hand in his pocket, produced a large writhing ball of worms and clay, and leered, It's like the inside of a giant golf ball, Miss. Want one?

But Shay Love's true value was that he knew things. For starters, he knew all about punk and he had once explained in the school magazine (where at great length he had rather aggressively interviewed himself) that punk was all about angry, honest songs of late seventies youth culture. And, as he quite rightly pointed out to himself, he was right too. He was right about most things.

But the problem for me, however, was that I wasn't part of youth culture – I was part of the Boy Scouts and the school choir and I didn't even know what to be angry about (apart from the Boy Scouts and the school choir). That is why I never became a vermivore like Shay Love and instead I just sat there waiting to be older, to be freer, to be grown up – for my own beard to grow and for my own voice to break. Only then would all those songs about fairies evaporate for ever. Only then would I be able to devote myself, with a clear conscience, to music and tall blondie-haired girls – in that order.

THE BOOK OF INVASIONS

'When you turn eleven or twelve you are trying to assert your individuality. Rock 'n' roll fulfils a specific function for everybody at that certain age. It's the one thing that really clicks with everybody no matter if you're in Indonesia or Russia. There's something about electric guitars, I guess.'

John Cale

Ceithleann of the Crooked Teeth lay dead against a chessie tree and the very birds, blasted by the density of her bad breath, were tumbling from the branches. The Battle of Moytura had been lost and Ceithleann's notorious husband, Balor of the Evil Eye, had been slain by his own grandson Lugh. It was the end of the Formorians and now the Tuatha Dé Danann were back as the rulers of the land. With this information and little else, myself and Spit Maguire headed off to Jamborora '77.

As part of the celebrations for a hundred years of the Boy Scouts in Ireland, a huge jamboree was held in Mt Mellary in County Waterford – a place where it was said that the monks slept in their own coffins. This was hardly a good sign, but even so, ten thousand Scouts were expected to arrive from all over the world in what would be Ireland's biggest ever mass pitching of tents, lashing of sticks and the unconvincing singing of jolly songs. It also promised both an open-air concert by Horslips and several tentloads of uniformed Girl Scouts from Sweden.

All Swedish women are rides, Spit assured me as he hissed off a spit into a bubbling drain. Every last one of them. That's a fact.

But I was not yet quite ready to engage with the notion of real women, especially Swedish women – even in Enniskillen I had heard stories about Sweden – so I panicked at the mere concept and changed the subject.

Horslips! I said quickly. Horslips are doing a concert!

'Ah, fuck Horslips! Spit snapped back. Sure can't you see them in Bundoran any day of the week. But you don't get too many big Swedish rides stepping about Roguey Rock in the buff!

I remained silent and examined the tarmac. I knew that he was certainly half right, and so I dwelt only on that part of it I could understand. Horslips did play regularly at the Astoria Ballroom but, being too young to go to dances, I never got to see them. Even so, I thought of little else.

On those long Friday nights of deprivation and despair I could only dream of all that dry ice drifting across the ballroom's bouncy floor and Horslips coming on stage to cheers and their chanted name, igniting Bundoran with lights you could see from the top of Lough Navar.

And then on Monday morning, the pointless,

wasted weekend spent, we would drape ourselves over the radiators in our soaking, steaming school uniforms and listen bitterly as prefects talked of 'Dearg Doom' and 'Trouble (with a Capital T)'.

But Jamborora had suddenly given me my chance. I was old enough to be let go to a Boy Scout jamboree and if Horslips were going to be there, well, I couldn't help that. And so it happened that a long-haired glam band called Horslips became an actual presence in my life and really did change everything for the better. Those Swedish Girl Scouts might well have saved me too, but I would never have got quite so close, quite so intimate.

At that Horslips gig I got myself right to the very front of the stage and I was as grateful as a boy could be. And Horslips didn't laugh or put me down, they smiled back and welcomed me to their glamorous Celtic world. And then when the show was over, I took a Horslips record home with me, brought it upstairs, examined it closely at my own speed and then played the very best bits of it over and over again.

Just a year before Jamborora, Horslips had released *The Book of Invasions*, a concept album based on a twelfth-century chronicle of the pre-Christian history of Ireland. It all sounds dodgy, certainly, but it was magnificent. With music based on traditional melodies, the record moved from the Fir Bolg to the Dé Danann to our friends the Formorians ('ancient enemies of cosmic order') and then through to the ultimate victory of the Sons of Mil at Tailteann in

County Meath. 'Honourable in defeat,' went the sleeve notes, 'the Tuatha retired to a hidden world parallel to ours where life, immortal, goes on as before.'

And so, at twilight Jamborora '77, with punk raging in London and Elvis Presley about to die in Memphis, our battlefield landscape of tents, flags and smoking fires began to boom with the sound of funked-up, rocked-up reels, jigs, set dances and marches. I faced into the setting sun, tied my neckerchief around my head and opened my arms wide to Barry Devlin's spine-trembling bass as it rumbled like escaping fear through my guts. It was glorious.

'Daybreak', then into 'Trouble (With a Capital T)', then 'The Power and the Glory' and I was right at the front, at Johnny Fean's feet – watching his fingers fly, Charles O'Connor's fiddle bow flash through the air, Jim Lockhart hunched over a whole city of keyboards and the skeletal Eamonn Carr, scary like one of the living dead, thundering behind the silvery kit – 'O'Neill's March' mixing with 'Shaft' and turning into 'Dearg Doom' and 'Toss the Feathers' crashing into 'Sword of Light' and 'The High Reel' and 'King of the Fairies' and the sound of a thousand valves opening up in my soul.

In some places, like Los Angeles or Seattle or Dublin perhaps, teenage boys were out buying electric guitars and muttering to each other about Humbucker pick-ups and Marshall amps. They were talking earnestly about Gibsons, and Rickenbackers and Strats and Telecasters – but not in my tiny universe, where a tin whistle was as rash as it could be.

They were suitably cheap, unambitious, unthreatening and asexual in brass or in chrome, Clarke's or Generation, and best in D and C. But the crucial thing was that if you could play a tin whistle even half well, then you could play 'Dearg Doom' and that meant you could play a Horslips tune – and that was the coolest thing I could ever imagine.

So soon my bedroom was the Astoria Ballroom itself, and I was up there throwing shapes with Barry, Charles and Johnny beside me, Jim in the distance to my left and, behind me, Eamon in his black string vest hammering away at the kit. I was suddenly, finally, able to leave, to travel, to escape as far as Bundoran and back and sometimes even further than that as I played along with records bought in Gannon's – a musical pharmacy which smelled of a million perfumes, aftershaves and rubbery hot-water bottles.

MERRY LITTLE TIT

'You know, before God threw him out, the Devil was
the chief angel in the choir.'

Clarence Fountain, The Blind Boys of Alabama

Ó'Dónaill's Dictionary offers many options for the
word *feis*. It means, among other things, 'sexual
intercourse' – a curious one given the rather less
juicy meaning it always had for us: a musical
gathering in the Technical College and the annual
opportunity to play tunes and win honour and glory
for St Gavin's – cups, shields, trophies and medals
with harps on them.

That said, it amounted to much more than just
another school imposition. It was an exciting and
thoroughly hormonal affair which we embraced
with some vigour, particularly as it tended to involve
a certain amount of awkward contact with the girls
from St Sinead's, who always arrived in an overwhelming rush of white – their probable curves well
hidden in long sexless dresses which turned them all
into walking triangles. The tall, skinny girls were
isosceles, the small, dumpy ones were equilateral and
then when they had finally arranged themselves
together on the stage, they seemed like the impreg-
nable snowy Alps.

A solid nun called Sister Frank acted as a shusher and a bouncer as the endless schedule of musical competitions got under way – our school pitted against theirs and prizes going first one way and then the other. And we thought we were great and we thought they thought we were great and we would snigger at their prim demeanour, their goofy smiles, their daft expressions as they sang with more emphasis on diction than on music.

In fact, at times, their rolling r's and volleyed t's were frightening – especially in a song about the coming of spring, where yearly they enunciated the line 'And she repeated it to a merry little tit' with so many percussive t's that you had to dive for cover behind Sister Frank. And every single year it cracked us up – the girls saying 'tit' with such precision and glee – and in many ways it was as thrilling as life could get.

But, apart from getting the odd girl in a half-hearted half nelson in among the duffel coats of the cloakroom, the Feis remained an entirely innocent affair. And we knew no other way. We were just clear-skinned boy sopranos with our school ties knotted tight around our heads in some Ninja ritual we had picked up at Jamborora – a sophisticated touch we believed made us irresistible. Yes, the Swedish Girl Scouts had been somehow immune to it but they were Swedish blondes after all. These triangular woman of St Sinead's could not afford to be quite so fussy. Or so we all hoped – especially Spit who was now all bumfluff and bluster and, as he kept putting it rather angrily, 'mad for it'.

So there we were – a choir of aspiring adults herded together by a priest and drilled into singing sad songs in Irish one minute, Gregorian chant the next, and then perhaps some rampant, lustful bit of an opera that reeked of wine and greasy beef. It was good stuff, most of it, and we were competent at singing it – all of it flowing out of us in a weird sinless sound that seemed to please just about everyone but ourselves.

But no matter what we were singing and despite instructions to watch the conductor at all times, our darting eyes kept lighting on that halted mountain range of white dresses at the door, those St Sinead's girls suddenly escaped and loose from the convent, tingling with dangerous detail – nail varnish, brace-lets, silver crosses and spearmint breath. I didn't quite understand any of it – but it was nice.

Spit was, by far, the quickest off the mark. He quit both the choir and the Scouts in one overnight attack and in less than a year he had managed to click in some hungry way with Madonna McManus. It took me a lot longer, however, and, medals or no medals, musical or miraculous, I soon began to realise that a boy soprano who played a tin whistle would never get anywhere. I was doomed, it seemed, to solitude, confusion and slow airs.

Have you ever heard of the castrati? asked Spit with some concern as we stepped on to the stage.

Of course I had not heard of the castrati. As Spit knew very well, I had heard of very little.

I have surely, I said, being at an age where I admitted no shortcomings.

That was some carry-on, eh? whispered Spit. What they did . . .

It was surely, I agreed vacantly.

The following Saturday morning I jooked into the library and uncovered the horrible truth about the castrati and plunged into a deep panic about why Spit had suddenly brought it up. I read on in some horror how St Paul had said it was a shame for women to speak in the church and how the sixteenth-century Vatican had decided it must also be a shame for them to *sing* in the church. And so young boys were enlisted to sing the women's parts – innocent and high. But this, of course, was only a temporary solution because a boy's voice was sure to crack during the terrible hurricanes of puberty and what would happen then? All that wasted effort, all those beautiful voices plummeting to croaks.

The only thing for it therefore was to 'modify' the boys' sexual organs, first to preserve and then to develop a soprano or contralto singing voice. And, duly 'modified', these new, perpetual sopranos became known as the castrati. I almost boked on the spot.

By 1640 they were singing in churches throughout Italy and by the end of the century they appeared regularly in opera. Their voices were more flexible than those of women and although composers like

Mozart and Monteverdi wrote parts specifically for them, it didn't make it any better for me as I turned the pages in growing pain. We had a few bad experiences with the Church's notions on a daily basis at St Gavin's but this was beyond all.

I read on. It said that Napoleon finally put a stop to it when his army invaded Italy in 1796 – the same year he half invaded Ireland. It was only then that this practice of castration ended for good, although many of the existing castrati went on to become the pop stars of the day – people like Farinelli who sang the same four songs every night for ten years and made women swoon whenever he climaxed with his famous high F.

In the 1800s, the choir of the Sistine Chapel was made up of eight basses, eight tenors, eight male sopranos and eight male contraltos and it wasn't until 1913 that the very last of the latter – Alessandro Moreschi – finally retired. And there was a record issued too, called *The Last Castrato – the Complete Vatican Recordings*, but it wasn't in the library's racks and I consoled myself with the probability that it wouldn't be in Gannon's either. There was every chance that I would never hear it and I certainly wasn't about to order it up.

Meanwhile, here was me still singing soprano in the school choir and heading for hormonal chaos. And what with other familiar voices beginning to shatter all around me, and my own surely about to go at any minute, the notion of the high voice quickly became inextricably linked to worrying questions of masculinity. And so the next few months were anxious ones — waiting, waiting, waiting — waiting and wishing my sweet-voiced life away and every single day I prayed hard to St Blaise, the patron saint of sore throats, that he might induce the fracture to come. It wasn't precisely his speciality but I was desperate and he was a saint.

By the following term, however, not only had I started to shave and grown about three feet in height, but the angelic voice too was away to Hell. I nervously demonstrated this obvious fact to our resigned and weary conductor and all he could do was issue a clinical nod and watch as another leaf fell off his big hedge of a choir.

And so I departed. It was all over and I stepped off the benches tiered high on the stage and left the choirs of angels for ever — discarded, rejected and suddenly beyond use. And as the gym door finally hushed closed behind me, I discovered that the tiniest smirk was beginning to curl across my lips. As I continued that long, relieved walk out of the choir and into my teens, I knew everything would be different from this moment on. No more medals, no more cups and no more songs about fairies. It was time to go electric.

FIAT LUX

'There was something about Horslips that Irish kids recognised as being theirs. We get lambasted regularly for loads of stuff – and rightly so for much of it – but the one thing that is undeniable is that we really did change for ever how people felt about their own culture. And the place where people really went bat-shit was the North.'

Barry Devlin

The town had gone through many changes since that distant day when Ceithleann had quietly expired at the East Bridge. It was Hugh Maguire – known as Hugh the Hospitable and not 'Hugh the Hospital' as a reporter on *Scene Around Six* had it – who first built a castle at Enniskillen and, by 1484, it was the undisputed capital of Fermanagh.

In 1508, O'Donnell of Donegal attacked with all his ragged force, and later, in the same year, O'Neill of Tyrone swooped and burned the place to the damp ground. Nineteen years on, Cuchonnacht Maguire rebuilt the ruined castle only for O'Neill to come back in a rage and install John II as chieftain. But of course that didn't last long either and soon he was replaced by Cuchonnacht II who then managed to remain in power for twenty-three long years.

The Maguire dynasty ended, however, with

another Hugh — son of Cuchonnacht II and the unfortunate last in the line. Elected chieftain in 1589, he was the one who chased England's sheriff back across the sea and told him not to come back near the place, but in the Nine Years War which followed, the castle changed hands between the Maguires and the English over and over again — lost in 1594, retaken in 1595 and then finally held until Hugh's death in 1600.

But then after all that effort of bloodshed and cannonballs, Hugh's successor, yet another Cuchonnacht, decided to destroy Enniskillen completely and clear off to Breffni, leaving the coast clear for the English who arrived in force and unopposed — led by an O'Donnell from Donegal. Between them they quickly demolished what was left and the social engineers of England began to dream up the new town of Enniskillen.

But as the century progressed this new Planter Utopia found itself up to its neck in revolts, upheavals and bother culminating in the Williamite Wars — various European powers battling it out in late seventeenth century backwaters like Derry, Aughrim, the Boyne and, of all places, Enniskillen. And from those who lined out for the curly-wigged Prince of Orange there grew the Royal Inniskilling Fusiliers and the Royal Inniskilling Dragoons — two famous regiments who took their mis-spelled name with them to places like Martinique, Grenada, Havana, Bergen, Egypt, Salamanca, Orthez, Waterloo, the Crimea, South Africa, Gallipoli, Suvla Bay,

St Quentin, the Marne, Richebourg, Ghent, Antwerp, Madagascar, India, Algiers, Sicily, Italy, Burma, etc., etc.

Fare thee well Enniskillen, fare thee well for a while,
And all around the borders of Erin's green isle,
And when the war is over, we'll return in full bloom,
And they'll all welcome home the Enniskillen dragoon.

The next landmark was the fire of 1695, which destroyed most of the town, and when they had put that out, another fire was lit in 1705 and the place was wrecked again. The eighteenth century saw Enniskillen recover and become much more prosperous with flax, yarn and linen for sale on The Diamond – the very spot where Spit Maguire would later spit at the punks. And soon, combined with the rural economy of the surrounding area, Enniskillen became a major garrison and market town. By the nineteenth century, Fermanagh butter was being exported as far as the West Indies, and Fermanagh cannon fodder was heading for slaughter all across the world.

Some of them had boots and stockings
Some of them had nothing at all,
Some of them had big bare arses
Coming back from the Crimean War.

And then there was cholera, scurvy, consumption and famine. The Great Famine in the middle of the century buried so many in bumpy mass graves, that we still walked quietly on; the rest were herded into the Union Workhouse to deal with fever in the dark. Between 1841 and 1851, over forty thousand Fermanagh people died – a quarter of the population.

But while the Maguires were no longer royal in their old kingdom, there were still plenty of them about. In fact, the place was full of them – the best known being Frank Maguire, the Member of Parliament for Fermanagh and South Tyrone; Hurd Hatfield (a Maguire), who starred in the movie of *The Picture of Dorian Gray*; Sean Maguire, the genius Belfast fiddler; Zammo Maguire, the schoolboy junkie on *Grange Hill*; the McGuire Sisters, who were like two female Pat Boones; Barry McGuire, who predicted in song 'The Eve of Destruction'; Sam Maguire, the sought-after trophy which Fermanagh could never win; Mary Maguire, the wife of the blind harper and composer Turlough O'Carolan; and Patrick Maguire of the Kavanagh poem. Then, of course, there were all the Maguires closer to home – Spit, Bart, Tarzan, The Swallow, and so on ad infinitum.

That said, they weren't what they used to be. The 1830s *Ordnance Survey Memoirs of Ireland* nutshelled it like this:

The name Maguire predominates in the town of Enniskillen. Though most of them move in a rather humble sphere, they take no small share of pride in tracing back their ancient lineage to the early lords of Fermanagh. Mr Thomas Maguire, ironmonger (according to his own reckoning), is the nearest heir to the forfeited title and estates of the last Lord Maguire, who was beheaded in London in the year 1644, and to the present day entertains strong hopes of their inheritance. These Maguires are exclusively Roman Catholic, though the respectable family of the same name, late of Tempo, are Protestant.

The first thirty years of the twentieth century brought many further changes to the Maguires and their descendants: the First World War, the Easter Rising, the Troubles, the Treaty, partition, electricity and the Great Depression – the last two arriving together in 1929. The next thirty years rushed in with the Second World War, the RAF, the US Army, rationing, smuggling, the end of rationing, the IRA's border campaign, Bill Haley and Elvis Presley. And then by the time I was thinking about being born, Enniskillen was a busy commercial town once again, flung along the length of its own main street – a great stone bridge to the east and the west.

I knew that to be a townie proper you had to be born between them, but by the time I landed, most births were taking place in the Erne Hospital just off the main island near the site of that old workhouse of 1845. On the day I popped out at the Erne in 1965, Dylan had released *Bringing It All Back Home* and was about to release *Highway 61 Revisited*, Sonny Boy

Williamson II had just blown his last on his harp and a barefoot Sandie Shaw was at number one with 'Long Live Love'. A month previous, the Beatles had been number one with 'Ticket to Ride'.

My home town, as I soon discovered, was now the county town of County Fermanagh, one of the nine northern counties of Ulster and one of the six which made up Northern Ireland. Fermanagh bordered Cavan to the south, Leitrim to the south-west, Monaghan to the south-east, Tyrone to the north and Donegal to the north-west – and all but Tyrone were in the South. It was a confusing state of affairs for any infant, muddled further because Donegal, while in the North, was also in the South i.e. the Free State, the Republic, the Twenty-Six Counties.

As northern towns went, it was by no means the most miserable and people, for the most part, were coexisting with good manners and restraint. We were, it seemed, a laid-back crowd – the consistently bad weather the probable cause of our easygoing and unambitious nature. Not much point in planning anything much when the next day was odds-on to be a wash-out, and so we learned early on that there was a certain comfort in expecting the worst, and a dull security in aiming rather low.

That said, we always had a few good days in the summer and even some pioneering tourists drifted in – Germans mostly, who arrived with leathery faces and yellow wellies to mingle with the Catholics and the Protestants, the Planters and the Gaels, the Townies and the Blow-ins, the Roughs and the

48

Toffs, the Rich and the Poor, the Corner Boys and the Culchies, the Drunk and the Sober, the Saints and the Sinners.

They came for the fishing and the undoubted delights of Lough Erne – the inland waterway which was at the very heart of the county and of the local psyche. Locals said that for half the year the Lough was in Fermanagh, for the other half Fermanagh was in the Lough. It had 365 islands – one for every day of the year – and it ran uphill from Lough Gowna in Longford as far as the Atlantic Ocean at Ballyshannon but most of it remained within the borders of Fermanagh – the Lower Lough in the north and the Upper Lough in the south – Enniskillen the strategic island where Upper and Lower met in a whirlpool of pike, perch, bream and confusion under the crucial bridges.

But by 1977, for all its rushes and reedbeds, its coots and kingfishers, Fermanagh was starting to lose its appeal. It just wasn't enough and although Spit, myself and Beckett knew it only too painfully, it took Floyd McAloon, just two years ahead of me at school, to articulate precisely what we were all thinking to the point of bitter rage.

He lived out in the townland of Coolisk – a damp raintrap more suitable for newts and frogs than it was for him. And although he went to Bundoran to see Horslips whenever he wanted, and although he had written poems about a girl who worked in the hotel, he had clearly seen enough of this particular watery corner.

You only live once, he announced with a big face on him, so why live in Coolisk?

It was the most profound thing I had ever heard. It was a statement and a question loaded with fact, challenge and possibility, and it put a sharp-edged shape on the dull chaos that was beginning to batter my brain from the inside out. And if there really was to be only one life to be lived, then yes – why? Give me two good reasons. Even give me one. Why would you want to live in Enniskillen? Or, for that matter, Ballycassidy, Agahalane, Teemore, Derrygonnelly, Drumskinny, Florencecourt, Garrison, Garvary, Roslea, Irvinestown, Tempo, Kesh, Killadeas, Kinawley, Belcoo, Bellanaleck, Belleek, Wattlebridge, Clabby, Killesher, Lisnaskea, Derrylester, Boa, Boho, Derrylin, Macken, Magheraveeley, Coa, Blaney, Maguiresbridge, Monea, Newtownbutler, Springfield, Lack, Lisbellaw, Letterbreen, Tamlaght, Tullyhoman or Whitehill?

*You lovers all both great and small, that dwell in
    Ireland,*
I pray you all pay attention while I my pen command,
It was my father's anger that drove my love away,
*But I still have hopes we'll meet again, in North
    America.*

*My love was fair and handsome and to him I gave my
    heart,*
And little was our notion that we would ever part,
It was in my father's garden that this flower it did decay,

But still I have hopes 'twill bloom again in North
    America.

I did not want for money, kind fortune on me shone,
And from my father's castle I stole five hundred pounds,
It was in the town of Belfast my passage I did pay,
My mind made up to follow my love into North
    America.

Now the captain's wife was kind to me as you may
    understand,
She kept me in her cabin until we reached dry land,
It was in the town of Quebec that we landed on the
    quay,
And I knew not where to find my love in all America.

But I being sick and sore and tired, I went into an inn,
And 'twas there I saw my William, the lad I loved
    within,
I took him gently by the hand and to him I did say,
I never thought to see your face in all America.

And now this couple have got wed as you may
    understand,
I hear they live quite happy in a town they call St John.
The money that she stole from home in gold she paid it
    down,
And she thinks no more on Ireland nor Enniskillen
    town.

REBEL REBEL

'The griots were historians, the people who were keeping the history. And the music is still playing the same role because it's the most effective way of communication. It is close to people. They understand the language, they understand the music and you can use it to send the message of history, the message of the future and also the message of today.'

Baaba Maal

In 1792, in an attempt to lure in the last remaining harpers from all over Ireland, prominent citizens of Belfast organised a harp festival in the city. Only eleven harpers showed up – the very last of the name – and most of them were ancient, lame, drunk and disillusioned. One of them wasn't even Irish.

The harpers had once been such a cherished and significant caste in Gaelic society that Elizabeth I had wanted them all hanged. She even issued a decree to that effect, understanding that one of the first steps in subjugation is to take the tunes out of people's hearts, the songs out of their throats and the history out of their heads. And while most of the harpers managed to escape the royal noose, they were to fade away even so, and by the end of the eighteenth century, their *raison d'être* entirely gone, they had become that ragged, wrecked company who turned up in Belfast in 1792.

And so this was the very last occasion on which they came together to perform. It was also, more fortunately, the very first time that their music was properly recorded – meticulously transcribed by a young pot-bellied organist from Armagh called Edward Bunting. Certainly their muted notes were no longer persistent with hope, but Bunting tailed the harpers anyway, cornering them, bothering them, buying them drink and ultimately saving all that was left of them. And in the dogged process, he also preserved what was once the art music of Gaelic Ireland.

A few years later, a violent rebellion, led by many of the same people who had listened to the last of the harpers in 1792, erupted out of the city's candlelit taverns and upper rooms. This largely Presbyterian conspiracy had first been ignited by the writings of Thomas Paine, by the French and American revolutions and perhaps by the same impulse that had prompted the Harp Festival. Before long, these music-loving revolutionaries were meeting in the busy merchant streets of Belfast to swear their oaths, make and accelerate their plans to secure early independence for Ireland – to create a republic which, it was intended, would unite Catholic, Protestant and Dissenter.

When Theobald Wolfe Tone, a young Dublin lawyer, secured the assistance of Napoleon for the Irish cause, everything suddenly seemed possible. All those Bastille Day celebrations had gone to many Irish heads and in 1796 a French invasion force of thirty-five ships and fifteen thousand men led by General Lazare Hoche headed unopposed to the south-west coast of Ireland.

The rebels waited and itched, anticipating the victory and the sheer shock. But Ireland being Ireland, disaster was certain to strike. An unexpected wind rose suddenly in the channel and the near revolution went off half-cock. The French were unable to land in sufficient numbers and, one by one, the struggling ships cut their lines and returned to France. Two years later, the one hundred thousand rebels of 1798 made yet another effort, thirty thousand of them were killed and the whole effort disintegrated in bloodshed, chaos and failure.

But, as teenage boys anxious for glamour and even a hint of sex, we sometimes imagined what it might have meant for our dull teenage lives if that wind had chosen not to rise and the French had managed to land in force and march triumphantly across the land. We were not necessarily contemplating the political upheaval, but rather the cultural one which would surely have hefted us out of both the parochial and the provincial in one stylish move.

Only for that wind we would not now be stuck with cub reporters on the local BBC talking about 'the mainland' and mispronouncing local place names. Instead, we'd be talking French and smoking Gauloise and Enniskillen would be Île de Cateleine – a beautiful spider's web of boulevards, grand public buildings, and people and things we had not yet heard of – Impressionist painters, philosophers, cognac and St Émilion. Chunky Rodin torsos would decorate The Diamond. Juliet Greco, Françoise Hardy and Serge Gainsbourg would be swinging their insteps at sidewalk cafés, and inside, standing at the dazzling brassy counters, beautiful, gorgeous, long-limbed, bouncy-breasted, slinky, sultry, sexy, seductive women would sip Pernod and smile out into the blue sunshine.

And then in the evenings we would perch at the Curly-Wurly Métro gates and watch flocks of fashion models emerge from the warm air of the Métro and into the breeze. They would smile and flick their hair, glide towards us like silky panthers and kiss us on both cheeks.

Salut, Chantale! Salut, Marianne! Salut, Françoise!

And then we would all go off and listen to jazz and talk about life. And what with all the champagne and the lovemaking, we would never ever get to sleep – delicious aches and comforts for days and glorious days.

But of course the French never arrived. Fermanagh remained Fermanagh and Enniskillen never became a Paris fragrant with coffee, Gauloise and girls. If only that wind had not decided to rise up in that seditious channel we would have had our own sexy little French Ireland, free from all the mind-setting bullshite that had us tied, fearful and without ambition or hope.

Irlande Érotique, Bart Maguire once replied to an

Où habitez-vous? from a confused French assistant at St Gavin's.

But I fear there is no such place, she shrugged sadly, gazing at Bart in total bewilderment.

Non, agreed Bart, admiring her hands as they caressed the creases in her forehead. No such place.

Non, she sighed aloud before checking herself with a sudden *alors!* and continuing with the class.

Of course, people in Northern Ireland had less and more than decadence and Sartre to worry about. There was, after all, a class of a war going on and the most you could hope for was that it would not come to your own door. What's more, it was something which was never going to end – a generally held opinion accepted as a further deathly inevitable. People therefore just worked out ways of living that suited them – established ways of going on that just about worked and got people through the day.

Of course, living in this way involved extraordinary skill, manners and diplomacy, and part of it related to what you sang and what you didn't. For instance, songs about 1798, like 'Boolavogue' or 'Kelly the Boy from Killane', were considered party songs and, as part of that incredibly delicate modus vivendi in Northern Ireland, people tended not to sing them – they might give offence and rise a row, and so it was best perhaps to store them in the prudent thatch of memory. 1798 wasn't all that long ago after all, even closer than 1690, and it was only in very mature mixed company that any kind of historical ballad might be aired even in fun. Otherwise, these were songs that only emerged in the repertoire of drunk men who had lost the run of themselves, or maybe people with death wishes for themselves or their neighbours.

And there were also other sober and sensible reasons for not singing them. Northern Ireland had become a very dangerous place and any facility for historical ballads might lead to all sorts of further assumptions about the singer of the song. A rebel song about 1798 might imply that the singer was some reincarnated Croppy subversive with pikes of his own hidden in the thatch, and the government, and others, were still very much on the lookout for people like that.

Paranoia ran deep in Northern Ireland, and with good reason too. It was very easy to end up on somebody's list and a party song was more than enough to promote you further up the list and into some very serious filing cabinet. A wise mother would constantly warn, Don't let anybody hear you singing that, you'll be lifted.

Not everybody thought like that. And while both sides had their party songs, only one side had to sing them either in secret or on holidays in the Free State. And while Luke Kelly was on Raidió Éireann singing 'Kelly the Boy from Killane' from a safe spot in Athlone, my little pal Nigel Johnston was outside singing another song entirely. Up and down, down and up, singing at the top of his voice in his long back garden of Sweet William and Orange Lily-O's.

His particular party song was not a subversive one, however. It was, rather, a straightforward and open expression of his absolute loyalty to the state we were all in. It was a song and a sentiment which made him belong and indeed he did.

He was singing an old ballad called 'The Sash My Father Wore' – an Orange anthem delivered with love, gusto or venom, depending on the singer. A Williamite hit, it refers with pride to Derry, Aughrim, Enniskillen and the Boyne – the various sites of Jacobite defeat back at the end of the seventeenth century. Therefore, it was sung by one side of the house only, i.e. the Protestant/Loyalist/Orange/ Williamite side. The other side – the Catholic/ Nationalist/Republican/Green/Jacobite contingent – would sing it only ever in mischief, or out of generous regard for its very fine melody.

Sure I'm an Ulster Orangeman, from Erin's Isle I came
To see my Glasgow brethren all of honour and of fame,
And to tell them of my forefathers who fought in days of yore,
All on the twelfth day of July in the sash my father wore.

(Chorus)
It is old but it is beautiful and its colours they are fine.
It was worn at Derry, Aughrim, Enniskillen and the Boyne;
My father wore it in his youth in the bygone days of yore
And it's on the Twelfth I love to wear the sash my father wore.

So here I am in Glasgow town youse boys and girls to
see,
And I hope that in good Orange style you all will
welcome me,
A true blue blade that's just arrived from that dear Ulster
shore,
All on the twelfth day of July in the sash my father
wore.

And when I'm going to leave yis all, 'Good luck!' to
youse I'll say,
And as I cross the raging sea my Orange flute I'll play;
Returning to my native town, to oul Belfast once more,
To be welcomed back by Orangemen in the sash my
father wore.

Nigel only seemed to know the chorus, but it was
always more than enough for me to realise that it was
certainly a loaded song. I cautioned him once, as his
best friend, that he'd be lifted if anybody ever heard
him singing it, but he was unmoved, confidently
replying that he would never, ever be lifted because
his uncle was a B-Special. And he was right about
that. It was a certainty he understood completely. In
fact, Nigel always seemed to know much more than
I ever did about the workings of this wobbly place in
which we both lived.

And so while he stamped on, proud and fearless,
up and down his garden singing about the sash his
father wore, I hunkered down and played solemnly
with the gravel. Yes, music could make you happy,
it could make you dance, it could make you stamp

your feet or it could even make you sleep, but I was now becoming aware that it could equally make you nervous and unloved. It could even make you afraid. It was the very first time that music had let me down.

And then when Nigel's endless singing would finally begin to boil my four-year-old blood in a shockingly fiery way, I would feel as if it was the music itself which was attacking me. He had twisted a good tune into something jeery and challenging and it would hurt my head like a stick – something which would send me back into the kitchen very uneasy indeed.

Then when July came around I would hear the same tune again. First, there would be an accordion band which would pass the house benignly enough. And then there would be a pipe band which would be alright too because we knew one of the bagpipers and he would look into the garden and wink from under his busby. But then, the third time, I would hear it coming for miles – drums rattling, battering, clattering – and it would make me shiver with the cold on the hottest day of the year.

It sounded like a giant was coming, leaping, bounding over the hills – angry and grim. His giant's boots were shaking the earth as he pounded along and he meant to do harm. It was Balor of the Evil Eye, of the Stout Blows, it was King Kong, it was Godzilla, it was the Cyclops or the Giant at the top of the beanstalk – *Fee fie foe fum, I smell the blood of* . . .

And then, one year, old Jonty 'The Scholar' Maguire, Spit's great-uncle, undertook to explain what it was all about. A soldier, he whispered, in King James's army was about to shoot King Billy but King James knocked the gun out of his hand and said, 'Don't shoot that man and leave my daughter a widow,' and then the Protestants bate the Catholics and James turned on his heels and ran. And then that's why he's called Jimmy the Shit. Anyway, that's the Protestants celebrating up the town now. Do you not hear all the bangin'?

And after all that news, I retired again to my own backyard to ponder in the coalhouse. I realised that my pal Nigel and all the Protestants and the B-Specials were up the town celebrating and that all the Catholics were at home, afraid of being lifted. And I waited, in silence, for all the music and the banging to end.

> *Oh! The French are on the sea,*
>   *Says the Shan Van Vocht;*
> *The French are on the sea,*
>   *Says the Shan Van Vocht;*
> *Oh! the French are in the Bay,*
>   *They'll be here without delay,*
> *And the Orange will decay*
>   *Says the Shan Van Vocht.*

OLD-TIME RELIGION

'God gives you the race! And God is love. Love and happiness.'

Revd Al Green

I was chewing at the toggles of my anorak; the tasteless plastic, the pressure on my tiny teeth, the spit-soaked string. Up the cold, stone spiralling steps to the gallery where my mother sang every Sunday and me standing beside her, chewing away, and listening to the beautiful, beautiful words – *miserere, laudate, aeternum, Dominooooooom.*

I loved the full, exaggerated vowels, the rolling r's, and the way the music seemed to be drawn so mysteriously from the mouths around me. These were all people I knew so well and they seemed such strange vessels for such supernatural sounds – the sudden expressions on their faces lit up with concentration, pleasure, awe, belief and deep amazement at the sheer beauty of it as the harmonies rose and fell – and the shivers on the back of the neck.

All eyes were on the conductor caressing the air in front of him as if conjuring the music itself. And Bart Maguire's grandfather played the extravagant organ and watched and prayed in a rear-view mirror as I sat beside him, my feet not touching the pedals and wondering at the complexity of it all – the huge wedding-cake bulk of it, the stops, the stop knobs, the piston knobs, the layers of plasticky keys.

And then there were the spilling boxes of loose pages, all tadpoles, frogspawn and Latin. *Ave Verum, Adoro Te, Panis Angelicus, Adoremus in Aeternum* and the church would fill with the most glorious music – sometimes quiet, sometimes sad, sometimes triumphant and always, even to a child vrooming his Matchbox cars along the seats, deeply moving. It lifted my tiny sparrow heart and put me right in the actual choir of angels. This was God's house and He certainly seemed to be in.

Sometimes I would watch the dots go by – up and down – trying to guess what the words might mean. Not that it really mattered because I must have understood even then that the vital process was one of feeling the music as much as singing it. When *Christus Vincit* was belted out you felt like cheering and punching the air. And *Stabat Mater dolorosa iuxta crucem lacrimosa* was sad like the deepest, weeping blues.

Whatever singing I ever did myself, I knew it was in a soprano voice and that when I grew up I would probably be a tenor – or maybe a baritone or a bass. I understood too that there were different parts to be sung and they came together in harmonies. I could hear that each part sounded incomplete on its own but that when they all swelled together, it was the most beautiful sound you could imagine. I heard names like Mozart and Gounod and I began to understand that music might be the most important thing on earth and maybe even further afield.

At then at Christmas someone would sing solo and their voices would actually lift you. Not just in a vague 'uplifting' sense but also in that more immediate sense that the wind would lift you. And it was so extraordinary, locally, to hear such drama and confident expression. In fact, it was almost shocking, because people weren't really like that. We were always such a muttering tribe who held back and stood back – reserved and guttural. And so this music was, for us, spectacular outside-of-ourselves stuff and it marked such gatherings well.

The Church marked all occasions well. In fact, it designed the very architecture of time for all of us, setting the milestones in our uneventful lives by way of sacramental ceremony – baptism, first confession, first communion and confirmation. The Sisters and Brothers coached us for everything, and along the way, we also rehearsed the eleven-plus. And then if we passed, we'd be handed over to the priests in the college for another seven years of it.

Some fuckin' prize! Spit would say.

Another stage in the Church's system for growth was joining the Scouts – again something which happened with a certain inevitability at the designated age. Perhaps it all seemed vaguely adventurous at the time, with its promises of travel to distant lands for white-water rafting, potholing, abseiling and endless jollity, but mainly, like the Church itself, we just became part of it without any actual thought or expectation. It was just another thing you did, something that happened to you, something that put a shape on your time. Even Spit enlisted, looking forward, he said, to spitting in campfires all around the world.

Leaving such things behind, however, would prove to be a much tougher challenge, where all the knots of loyalty and perception would have to be delicately picked at and loosened. And when that clifftop moment came, when you understood that you were not at all the person you (or other people) had thought you were, it took some little courage to shed the skin, the uniform, the reputation, the image, the approval and the illusion.

Yes, it was letting everybody down to do so – parents, aunts, uncles, neighbours, curates, parish priests, the parish, the estate, the town, the county, the diocese and the country – but it had to be done and it took a nerve I did not yet have. Spit of course was different. He was ahead of me as usual and he was the first of us to coldly desert and take all the consequences.

I'm not fuckin' collecting any more fuckin' money for any more fuckin' charity walks. If I have to ask my mother to fuckin' sponsor me one more fuckin' time, she'll fuckin' kill me. And she'd be fuckin' right! And what the fuck am I wearing a uniform for? Does John Travolta wear a uniform? He does like fuck!

My wise pal Bart departed shortly afterwards.

I feel foolish, he said, singing that song about the

man with the dog called Bingo and the other one about never getting to heaven with Brigitte Bardot, whoever she may be. There is no future in it. We are future hens.

And then when I finally left myself, the reasons were simple. Firstly, Shay Love had never been in the Scouts and he was the coolest person I knew, and secondly, wearing a uniform of any description was not compatible with me being into Horslips. And so I took a deep breath and decided that, whatever the consequences, whatever horrors it would ignite in those who thought me a prime Scout for life, I would have to rip off that woggle, yank away that lanyard and loosen up.

The time had come for major reinvention. There were new and tastier glories to be discovered and, to find them out, I needed to be my own teenager, make my own moves, clear my own space, locate my own future and most importantly walk the scary plank into the here and now. I realised too that I simply could not, for one screaming moment longer, bear to be a grown-up's idea of what a nice young boy should be.

> *Oh you'll never get to heaven*
> *With Brigitte Bardot*
> *'Cos Brigitte Bardot*
> *Is going below.*

Maybe so. But I decided to chance it.

HOLY THURSDAY

'I had conversations with Geldof years ago and he was saying, look, Bono, back in your box . . . rock 'n' roll, pop music . . . accept it for what it is, it's never gonna change the world; if you're lucky it'll change the temperature of the room. But I just didn't believe that. I believe that there's something sacramental about music and I really believe in its power to change things.'

Bono

Myself and Spit just kept on trying to pin down the present — something which finally began to take shape when we heard the ridiculous rumour that Thin Lizzy were coming to town.

There's no fucking way, reasoned Spit. Not a chance in hell.

Well, I insisted, somebody saw a poster beside Tunney's Meat Packers and Bart Maguire ripped it down and he has it in his house.

What the fuck, continued Spit, methodically pausing for emphasis, would Thin Lizzy . . . be doing . . . playing . . . in Enniskillen? Are you are mad? . . . or what?

Well, I'm going down to Bus Stop after school to look for a ticket.

Catch yourself on! Thin Lizzy? In Enniskillen? Your head's a fuckin' marley!

We were both, by this stage, obsessive Thin Lizzy fans and the thought of them actually playing live right in the heart of the Fermanagh void was certainly, as Spit kept putting it, 'in-fuckin-credible'. But the rumours were true. Bart brought the poster into school and soon we had all swapped a fiver for a bright pink ticket. We read and reread what it now said in bald, bold print. It seemed far too much like a dream.

McCANN/DESMOND
present
THIN LIZZY
FORUM, ENNISKILLEN
THURSDAY, 3 APRIL
Doors open 7.30 p.m.
Official Thin Lizzy merchandise available in the
Hal [*sic*]
Unreserved £5.00
No. 516
To be Retained. Tickets cannot be exchanged
or money refunded.

This was without question the most exciting thing ever to have happened in our lives and, as the date approached, we were distracted and sleepless.

They'll only play for twenty minutes, cautioned Bart Maguire. That's what these bands do. God knows and my nose knows. You ask my nose and it'll tell you. Lakeland Forum, Lakeland Boredom, Whoredom, Snoredom . . .

The word 'Lakeland' offended Bart Maguire. It riled me too. It was one of the buzzwords the town burghers employed to make the lough sound less uncouth. Suddenly, everything in the county was called 'Lakeland' this and 'Lakeland' that – something designed to attract the tourists with its echoes of the Lake District and it was just one of a long list of words that we refused to use on principle – *mainland*, *gorse* and *absolutely* being the main ones. The Lakeland Forum we just referred to as 'the complex'.

Ah, fuck away off! Spit once shouted at a lifeguard who told him not to spit in his new turquoise pool. We had a complex in this town long before you bastards, fuckye!

But we spent every Saturday there, hunched over the Space Invaders machine, drinking 7-Up and playing indoor soccer. There was also a vague girl thing going on too, as nervy huddles of them in multicoloured windcheaters watched us kick the ball around – something which was oddly agreeable in a way it had never been before. But the most important thing now, more important than indoor soccer, or Space Invaders, or the whispering girls, is that Thin Lizzy were coming to play in the complex. A real band. Our favourite band. Thursday, 3 April 1980 would be the day I would leave the house in a brown cardigan and come home in a creaking leather jacket.

But first I had to go to Mass. Thursday, 3 April was Holy Thursday – a Lenten peak and Lent was a serious business. It meant no sweets, no buns, no 7-Up, no sugar in your tea and plenty of Mass. On Holy Thurdays Mass was at five in the afternoon and it was a long affair. And this Holy Thursday would be no different. End of story. Before there would be any Thin Lizzy, there would be Mass, and plenty of it.

And so there I was, stuck in a solemn moment of fidelity from which there could be no early escape. Spit was halfway up the church, trying hard not to forget himself in God's house. Bart was a few rows behind, standing with his head in his hands, and Shay Love was at the back, by the holy water barrel – the Botticelli he called it – all on his own, and wearing a spectacular new haircut of his very own design. I was also standing alone – at that crucial age when the greatest statement of individuality open to us was to go to Mass without our mothers and fathers.

Time dragged slower than usual and all I could do was watch in pain as the minute hand completed its endless taunting circuits of my black-faced Sekonda watch. A clash was certainly beginning to bubble between the old ways and the new, and even though I didn't know what it all meant, I began to feel all sorts of new impatiences tingling on my scalp. I shifted and shuddered – one foot on the kneeler in front of me, then the other as I dug my fingernails into the shiny thick varnish of the pew. My back began to ache and sweat and I sighed aloud through gritted, anxious teeth.

And in a way the Church itself was to blame for its

eventual defeat. It wasn't the clergy of my own parish who were actually responsible, because they were strangely oblivious to Thin Lizzy and knew nothing about the gig at all. It was in fact the parish priest of Bundoran who had apparently made the pivotal move. The rumour was that he had questioned the appropriateness of a Thin Lizzy gig at such a crucial Lenten moment − this was Holy Thursday after all − the Agony of Jesus in the Garden and all the disciples dozing and dreaming of the open sea. And so, we were told, he barred Thin Lizzy from his Donegal turf and the whole thing was then moved to our godless complex over the border.

And so I kept looking at my watch. Over and over again, I kept glancing slyly at time itself; gauging the hands for movement, sighing, then checking again. It was a watch my father had bought for me when I finally reached the age of seven − a theologically charged age which meant that you were entitled to the timepiece of your choice. I picked a Sekonda with a black face. I strapped it on and wore it like a proud tattoo.

According to the school catechism, seven was the age when young boys and girls reached the age of reason. It meant that they now knew, for sure, the difference between right and wrong and so were expected to act accordingly. It was a serious border checkpoint at the land of sin − and from here on you were expected to wander alone armed only with the grace of God, an informed conscience and a well-wound watch.

And so from 27 June 1972 onwards, there would be no excuses for anything; all my sins would have to be ticked, weighed, measured and confessed – a business so tricky that maybe a high-quality calculator might have been a more appropriate gift. But I was glad of the watch even so – happy to know the time of day and my place within it. It was a powerful symbol of the times ahead and of the many moments to come; all of them now suddenly comprehensible, manageable, measurable and all grown-up.

I loved it – the worn leather strap sliding on my bony wrist like a bangle, and only for an extra hole punched with a compass it might easily have fallen down a bubbling Enniskillen drain, something which would have been a shocking disaster. This irreplaceable thing was already an heirloom. It represented not only my status as a little man, but also all kinds of ties to my own particular holy family – an early shackle of responsibility but one gratefully accepted even so.

I had chosen it for three grown-up reasons:

1. It had a black face.
2. The hands glowed in the dark.
3. It was made in Russia.

These were all great reasons and even when the boys from swanky families got their new digital watches – huge, bulky, silvery manacles that beeped and flashed – I hung on to my streamlined Sekonda with pride. It didn't tell the time in Hong Kong and America but I knew there was something far more enduring about my Communist watch with its green, glowing hands and the letters USSR curving around its edge. It was compact and classy and I looked at it faithfully and with reverence day and night.

And so as the minutes stretched that Holy Thursday, my black-faced watch seemed as big as the universe, marking relentless time in terms of huge tangible experience rather than all those lame *one Mississippi two Mississippi* seconds – a strange sensation only to be experienced underwater or in the middle of a big yawn. The actual architecture of time was of course something I had known nothing about because I had no music of my own. No record player and no three-minute singles to mark and pass the moments.

But this was an extraordinary day. Normally, in Enniskillen in 1980, there was no real need ever to check your watch. Nothing either happened or was about to happen, and apart from home time at half three, and indoor soccer on Saturday, there were few glorious moments to the twenty-four-hour cycle. Everything was marked simply by school bells and television programmes. If *News at Ten* was on, you might as well be in bed. If you heard 'O'Donnell Abú' chiming on an RTE radio xylophone, it was time to get up again. At fourteen, that was all there was. There were no appointments, no rendezvous, no showtimes and no hot dates.

But today was different and there were others checking their timepieces also – Spit squinting at his tiny Timex, Bart at his ancient and permanently stopped pocket watch, while Shay Love, who refused to wear a watch on some kind of principle, repeatedly consulted with a grumpy old lady in front of him.

Occasionally we caught each other's eyes through the bowed heads and impatiently we acknowledged our frustrations with a theatrical shrug or a raised eyebrow. And by the time Father Monaghan finally squeaked that we were free to go in peace we were already very far away. There was something happening, something dangerous and entirely delicious.

> *The boys are back in town*
> *Get your knickers down . . .*

INTERLUDE

'It's such a primeval thing – it's right within the human soul. The animal man has been making music for at least eighty thousand years and we know that for sure because of discoveries of fragments of little flutes and so on. Actually, I think man sang before he talked. It's such an essential part of our lives. I don't know what I would have done without music. I can't imagine a world without it.'

Sir George Martin

When Fionn Mac Cumhaill set about wresting the leadership of the Fianna from Goll Mac Morna, he knew well that he had his work cut out for him. He had already proven himself a poet, a scholar, an athlete and a giant of a man, but leadership of the Fianna was another matter entirely and the ultimate honour for any Irish warrior.

And so, full of spunk and bullshit, Fionn Mac Cumhaill headed for Tara, gatecrashed a banquet, sat down beside the High King and pledged his allegiance. The King, who had known and respected Fionn's father, laughed at his cheek, welcomed him and made sure he was properly fed and watered. Wine was poured, beef was carved and his gnarly feet were anointed with oils and herbs.

But as the night went on, however, it became

clear that the royal court of Tara had much on its mind. It was the eve of the festival of Samhain – the day when the gates of the otherworld flew open and the Tuatha Dé Danann re-emerged to walk among mortals. Fiercest among them was the monstrous musician Aillen Mac Morna who, every Samhain, came to Tara and burned it to the ground. The Fianna were powerless against him and so all they could do was to wait, impotently, for the coming day with ever-darkening gloom.

Aillen Mac Morna was no ordinary demon and his power lay entirely in his music. With the enchanted notes of his tiompán, he would lull the entire court to sleep – guards, warriors, the Fianna, the Druids, the dogs, the cattle, the fowl and even the King himself. Nothing alive was immune from the power of Aillen's music and with Tara soon deep in sleep, he would launch a huge bolt of fire from his throat, ignite the royal ramparts and burn the palace to ashes and dust.

But Fionn was young and eager and he was not afraid. Confidently, he announced that he himself would save Tara, on condition that the King would guarantee him one thing – leadership of the Fianna. The King, being desperate, agreed and Fionn immediately set about defeating both the music and the magic, seeking the help his father's old ally Fiacha.

Fiacha was a good man to know. He had a magic spear which he gladly gave to Fionn with the words, 'As soon as you hear the evil music, unsheathe this spear and place the blade against your forehead. It will keep you awake and that way you will overcome the sorcery of Aillen.'

And so Fionn took his magic spear to the ramparts of Tara and began his watch. Sure enough the music soon began to drift in from the distant foggy blackness and, at once, Fionn held the blade of Fiacha's spear against his forehead, waiting for the first sight of the demon Aillen. And as the music filled the halls of Tara everyone quickly fell into the deepest slumber – everyone except Fionn who stood silent and still, watching and waiting.

Once Aillen thought he had lulled everyone to sleep, he began to sneak out of the fog. Fionn watched as suddenly the demon rose up in the air and opened his awful mouth, sending a river of flame straight across the plain towards the royal court.

But then the watchful Fionn jumped out and using his great cloak he deflected the fire deep into the earth. Aillen was shocked and terrified and immediately he turned and began to flee at great speed back to his underground fort. But Fionn was quicker again, and hurling his magic spear he watched it follow the demon through the air, gaining on him constantly, as he tried to outrun his doom. And indeed Aillen was no match for Fionn and his spear, and just as he reached his fort, the great weapon pinned the writhing demon to his door.

The next morning, Tara awoke in the purple light to find Aillen's head impaled on a pole. Fionn had done it. And a great cheer went up that was heard as far away as Norway. There would be no more enchanted music and Tara was saved. And so, as Fionn handed over the magic tiompán of Aillen, he claimed his due reward — leadership of the Fianna — and embarked on a long career of heroic feats and superhuman deeds.

During breaktime, I was Fionn Mac Cumhaill and Spit was Aillen Mac Morna, howling out his enchanted music and spitting what he imagined was a river of fire at the gable wall of the dinner hall. And then at intervals I would spring up and hurl a stick at him as he ran for cover. In my mind my magic spear would impale him against the classroom door, and then I would carry his startled head back into class to show the giggling nun.

IRELAND'S OWN

'Anywhere that was anti-showband, we would play.'

Rory Gallagher

When Gerald of Wales wrote his *Topographica Hiberniae*, he paid the following backhanded tribute to the skill of Irish musicians:

I find among these people commendable diligence only on musical instruments, on which they are incomparably more skilled than any nation I have seen. Their style is not, as on the British instruments to which we are accustomed, deliberate and smooth but quick and lively; nevertheless the sound is smooth and pleasant.

But the problem, however, is that Geraldis Cambrensis never saw a showband. The year was 1185 and the showband tribe had not yet appeared on the Irish landscape with their shiny suits and their swinging saxophones. More specifically, Seamie Sheridan had not yet been born and there is no doubt that if Geraldis had encountered him on his travels, his *Topographica Hiberniae* would have had an altogether different slant.

Sheridan had a band called the Shamrock Show-band, known simply as the Shamrock, until he decided, unaware of the implications, to shorten it to the SS. Then in later years, as his head got yet bigger, he added his own name and the complete title became the tongue-twisting Seamie Sheridan's Shamrock Showband. Even at primary school Spit was already challenging all comers with it: *She says shite Seamie the sham's shite Shamrock Shiteband are a shite showband sham.*

And so with his brand-new van decorated with a giant shamrock and the words 'Seamie Sheridan's Shamrock Showband' (the SS) on the side, this creepy unmusical creature lived out his nocturnal, cash-only existence on the roads and lanes of the county – always on his menacing way to or from a dance.

But shite is not quite the word for the SS. You simply could not listen to them. Technically, it was not an actual showband – or a band of any description for that matter – because all it amounted to was Seamie Sheridan's eight fat fingers and a drum machine permanently stuck in waltz time. But as far as myself and Spit were concerned, showband or not, it was a deeply embarrassing sub-culchie horror and it made us sick to our stomachs. We grew to hate Seamie Sheridan, and what he represented, with a hatred that was pure and there were nights when we might easily have killed him in some cruel and unusual way.

At school I had learned that a waltz was a three-in-a-measure dance which had gained popularity at the end of the eighteenth century. Its harmonic characteristic was one chord per measure with the bass note on the first beat and the rest of the chord on the other two — *one-two-three, one-two-three, one-two-three*, and so on. In the lumpy hands of Seamie Sheridan and the SS, however, it was just a constant *bum-chicka-chicka, bum-chicka-chicka* which went on for hours, days, lifetimes on end.

There was no tune in existence that Seamie Sheridan could not force into the mechanical rhythm of his waltz, most of them sentimental songs of the genre known as country and Irish — head–bealding stuff about local places, all sung in a very bad American/west Ulster accent.

Thangyews verra much, Seamie Sherdian would say. *Fir me nixt number ah'd lek tee sang a bid uv a wee medleee dere . . . Kyenny Rahgers . . . 'Caaaar duv the Cownee' . . . ahn 'The Flaaar uv Sweed Strabayan' fur the mizziz who's fram Strabayan and all belonging tee her . . . ahn a liddle sang by Dactar Hyook . . . Thangyews. Ivrybady aht ahn the flur fir a good old tahm walls . . . wan two, wan two . . . testin' testin' . . . ho kyeh . . . hee-yur wi go nah . . . wan tew tree . . . wan tew tree . . .*

But whatever the musical and personnel limitations of the SS, Seamie Sheridan actually had been in a showband and had therefore been an actual bit player in the Showband Era — the period now remembered with either affection or shame, depending on who you talked to. It was, however, a reasonable assumption that any era that could spawn somebody like Seamie Sheridan was better off over.

Certainly myself and Spit were glad we had missed it – the dickied-up showbands knocking out number after number for the jiving multitudes all tanked up on minerals and sugary tea as the crooner eyed the takings piling up in the biscuit tin at the door. It seemed grotesque – the lumpy dance routines, the Pioneer Pins, the pills, the parish priest rubbing his hands, the bishop sitting at home watching the clock for midnight and his Cinderella curfew.

That said, the showbands were hugely popular and they played to thousands every night of the week. But then when the sixties finally arrived in Ireland (at the start of the seventies), the showbands began to crash and Seamie Sheridan, and people like him, began to get bitter and grim. He began to hate everybody younger than himself, in particular the Beatles because, as he saw it, they had stolen his gig. Only for them, thought Seamie Sheridan, he'd have been a far bigger star than he thought he already was. And the Beatles were all hype, he used to say every time he got drunk, and they couldn't play for shite.

But the Showband Era wasn't all about bad music played by gobshites. While Seamie Sheridan was touring the ballrooms and tea-stained sugar tins of Ireland, Enniskillen sprouted a showband of its very own. They were called the Skyrockets and they had a guitar player called Henry and he really did like music. He liked the Beatles too.

Henry McCullough was the first person on Derrin

Road with long hair, and while Seamie Sheridan festered away in some jivey parallel ballroom, Henry started to connect with what was really happening in the rest of the world. And so, guitar under his oxter, he buggered off in search of it.

Then picture the scene one night in the late seventies when I'm sitting at home with my mother half watching the television and contemplating my boredom and Wings are on BBC1 playing a concert. I didn't like them much, but at least they had long hair and they were jumping about so I left it on – Paul McCartney's eyebrows reaching for the high notes and Linda tapping on the keys.

Ah, there's Henry, said my mother in a very matter-of-fact way.

Henry who? I said, glancing towards the venetian blinds.

On the television, she said, nodding to the box between us.

No, Ma, that's Paul McCartney, I sighed.

I know that's Paul McCartney, said my mother, but that's Henry with him.

Henry who? I snapped.

Henry McCullough! she said as if I should already know. I see he never got his hair cut anyway . . .

And who's Henry McCullough when he's at home? I sniggered, sneering at the apparent absurdity of this conversation.

He used to be in the Skyrockets, said my unflappable mother, or was it Gene and the Gents? He was in one of them anyway. I think the

Skyrockets was before Gene and the Gents . . . maybe he was in the two of them. Him and Cecil Kettyles.

By this stage I thought that my mother was actually doting and I reminded her that what we were watching on television was Paul McCartney, formerly of the Beatles, playing with his new band called Wings. It had nothing whatsoever to do with anybody called Henry who played in a band called the Skyrockets with Cecil Kettyles. Catch yourself on, Mother, I thought.

But she was right. It was true. Henry McCullough was in Wings and my mother knew Henry McCullough and Henry McCullough knew Paul McCartney. It was news which was beyond all believing, and in some way it affected everything. In fact, nothing was quite the same again once I had discovered that somebody could move from Planet Derrin Road to Planet Paul McCartney on the television with long hair and an electric guitar. Prior to the Henry McCullough revelation, such things were totally and absolutely unthinkable.

And then yet more bizarre discoveries began to tumble into the curious grating on the top of my head. Tom Thumb had visited Enniskillen in 1871, de Valera had stayed on The Long Road when he was on the run, Eisenhower and Patton had gone past the front door in a jeep during the war, King Leopold of the Belgians was at Mass one Sunday, the Dubliners had played a gig at the Ritz, the Troggs, Millie and Roy Orbison had played somewhere else.

Floyd Patterson had been in the town too and he got his picture in the *Fermanagh Heron*.

Yet more investigation revealed that one of the Bee Gees was married to a Fermanagh woman, that Josef Locke had been a policeman in the town and that Joan Trimble had played piano for John McCormack. But the biggest thunderbolt of all came when Bart Maguire's father suddenly muttered, with no provocation at all, that John Lennon was Bart's second cousin.

You mean to tell me, spluttered Bart, that John Lennon is my second cousin and I'm only hearing this now!

Man dear, lower your voice, barked his father, people will hear you.

John Lennon is my cousin! screamed Bart.

Second cousin, his father huffed back.

The John Lennon? The Beatles and the granny specs? persisted Bart.

Aye, sighed Mr Maguire, and he's some playboy, that fella.

John Lennon! screeched Bart. You're saying that John Lennon is my cousin?

Don't raise your voice to me, cub! shouted Bart's father, regretting the information he had leaked. And haven't you enough cousins?

And so it was with great excitement and care that these curious and extraordinary drops of information were gradually mixed, shaken and distilled into something like an antidote for living in the way we did. And now as we sat, as usual, under lamp-posts on wet nights, we tipped at our new and developing truths – all of them swigged with pinches of salt and a growing sense of wonder.

CLEARING THE AIR

'It seems to me that a lot of the white kids know more about the music than a lot of the black adults. And that's fine with me because I want the white kids to know about it and I'm glad somebody knows about it! But I wish young blacks would take more interest. I don't necessarily want black kids to like the blues, I wish they would, but I just want them to know about it. It worries me quite a bit.'

B.B. King

When I was a baby boy, long before Horslips and Thin Lizzy, I was often found playing with clock beetles under the kitchen table and listening to Louis Armstrong on the radio. He was always singing 'Hello Dolly' and I liked it very much. I had arrived to the strains of it and it had stuck – an overly casual midwife who couldn't get the first line out of her head had sung it repeatedly as I resisted being born. Then there was Sandie Shaw, the Bachelors and, my real favourite, Dusty Springfield. But mostly I just heard my mother singing 'Mairzy Doats and Dozy Doats' or my father humming 'For Love is Pleasing' and this was the first music I ever heard. My uncle Frank Lydon always sang Slim Whitman songs but people usually stopped him before he really got going and it was just as well. He used to cry as he sang and it frightened me.

Because we had no record player in the house I had to get all my music from the radio – beginning with that hypnotic xylophone version of 'O'Donnell Abú' played every cold pitch-black morning, a strange repetitive spacious signal drifting up from Athlone in the cold morning air. I often wondered who the man was who was playing it – sitting there freezing morning after freezing morning, hunched over his little xylophone, his mug of black tea steaming in the darkness and him tap, tap, tapping as the notion took him.

Without Raidió Éireann there would have been no music at all. But for Ciarán MacMathúna and *The Lark in the Clear Air* and whatever he chose to play, we would have heard nothing. Enniskillen was, after all, not some rural Babel of music and song. There were no fiddlers like Johnny Doherty arriving at our place to hammer out tin cans and then play all night as dancers kicked up sparks around our kitchen hearth. There were no pipers, no box players, no scrapers and no lilters to keep us up till dawn. There were no singers to settle in at the range, put their caps on their knees, warm their shins and launch suddenly, after long protest, into forty-verse ballads loaded with Greek gods and ornamentation. We had none of that – only what leaked in on the wireless like precious oxygen.

But out in places like Mulleek everything was

different. The singer Paddy Tunney was in somebody's kitchen, commanding attention in a house
surrounded by wet fields and singing 'Lough Erne
Shore', the neighbour's dog breathing heavy on the
lino as verse after verse tumbled out.

> One morning as I went a-fowling
> Bright Phoebus adorned the plain;
> 'Twas down by the shores of Lough Erne,
> I met with this wonderful dame.
> Her voice was so sweet and so pleasing,
> These beautiful notes she did sing;
> The innocent fowl of the forest
> Their love unto her they did bring.
>
> It being the first time I saw her,
> My heart it did lep with surprise
> I thought that she could be no mortal,
> But an angel who fell from the skies.
> Her hair it resembled gold tresses,
> Her skin was as white as the snow
> And her cheeks were as red as the roses
> That bloom around Lough Erne Shore.
>
> When I found that my love was eloping
> These words unto her I did say
> O take me to your habitation,
> For Cupid has led me astray.
> For ever I'll keep the commandments,
> They say that it is the best plan
> Fair maids who do yield to men's pleasure,
> The Scripture does say they are wrong.

O Mary don't accuse me of weakness,
For treachery I do disown
I'll make you a lady of honour,
If with me this night you'll come home.
O had I the Lamp of Great Aladdin,
His rings and his genie, that's more,
I would part with them all for to gain you
And live upon Lough Erne Shore.

But that kind of thing only happened in places like Mulleek, and The Long Road was another universe entirely. In towns like Enniskillen, what passed for Irish music was mainly the odd blast of John McCormack, a parlour song perhaps, maybe music-hall material or, more often than not, some polite stagey stuff like Percy French – 'Phil the Fluther's Ball', with all the winking and thigh-slapping that went along with it. *Begorra! Mrs Cafferty, yer leppin' like a hare!* Etc., etc. Any amount of that guff but never the actual thing itself.

But then one summer's night when I was out mooching about – just me and my deflated football – I was attacked by the most exciting, satisfying sound I'd ever heard. It was a warm, slow evening and all the windows in the estate were wide open to midges and daddy-long-legs. I was listening to the televisions blaring from some houses, the odd row from others, when suddenly a brand-new excitement burst out the living-room window of Dan McManus's house and rushed my body and soul. It was the Bothy Band and it almost knocked me down.

I knew nothing then about instruments or arrangements but this was the most alive music I had ever heard. I discovered later that it was the left hand of Donal Lunny chopping at a bouzouki that was driving it along with such power, that it was the left hand of Tríona ní Dhomhnaill which was hammering out a bassline on the clavinet. But at first hearing, it was just sheer volume and power.

Together with pipes and flute and fiddle and guitar, it sounded like the wind, or like a thunderstorm in my own heart. It felt like flying in the middle of a giant flock of birds, or like diving into a roaring wave. Whatever it was, it was the sound of some euphoria I had not yet discovered and I ran as hard as I could to Spit's back door, leaping the gate, falling, and then rapping the door as hard as I could with my new white knuckles.

Come on quick till you hear this! C'mon before it's over!

Where are we going? shouted Spit impatiently, half a sandwich still in his mouth. It better be somebody topless or something!

Dan McManus's.

What the fuck for?

There's music coming out of his house and I don't know what it is. It's like . . . I don't know what it's like . . .

Ah, for fuck's sake . . . you're such a tube so you are.

And so we stood against the gable wall of Dan

91

McManus's house and I listened and looked at Spit for confirmation.

What about that?! I begged. Have you ever heard anything like that in your life?

It's a fuckin' céilí band! said Spit indignantly.

That's not a céilí band. That's better than any céilí band.

Where's me knickers, I'm going home, moaned Spit.

But this is amazing! I persisted.

Well, it's not fuckin' Motörhead! snapped Spit.

It's far better than feckin' Motörhead! I shouted angrily.

Ballocks! Spit shouted back, directing his chin at me.

That music, I said, shoving him in the shoulder, is far feckin' heavier than feckin' Motörhead!

And so we fell out again. Spit returned sullenly to his new loves of Black Sabbath and AC/DC and Motörhead and I started to investigate what I had just heard shake the summer air. The next day in town I realised that this music – the Bothy Band, Planxty, the Chieftains, Paul Brady and Andy Irvine – was all right under my nose and for sale in one corner of Gannon's.

And so the music continued to arrive piece by piece, link by link. Pipes, fiddles and flute all connected immediately with something deep and reassuring. It was as if condensation was clearing on a window and the new view was something I had somehow seen before. And then it turned out that

Paul Brady had cousins in Irvinestown and that we knew Donal Lunny's cousins too, and on and on it went.

And here too was a music which had nothing to do with school, with winning medals, or with politeness. We had certainly glanced against it at St Gavin's but now here it was for real and it couldn't be cooler. What's more, it was my own, connecting me at once to the past, to the future and, most importantly of all, to the present. Stravinsky was right and, not for the first time, Spit Maguire was wrong. The big ballocks.

PLUGGED

'Anybody can play those three or four chords – anybody
– I don't care who you are. We can all take a swing at it.
It's a democracy.'

Lou Reed

And so, friends again after I broke the silence with
the John Lennon news, Spit and I formed a group –
not a traditional group because Spit wouldn't hear of
it – but a bedroom rock band which would never
actually leave the house. Spit played acoustic guitar
and I wielded an electric bass – a Fender copy and a
crock of shite which had cost my entire life savings
of £35. But because I couldn't afford an amplifier,
and there was no room for one anyway, I was
doomed to remain unplugged and literally unheard
of.

The music I made on that lifeless, but perfectly
shaped, bass guitar was no more than the dull twang
of cable but it didn't really bother me. The
important thing was simply to wear the instrument –
settle the strap on my shoulder and pretend to be
Phil Lynott. I put my foot up on the monitor I didn't
have and I mimed along to the records, throwing the
most impressive of rock-star shapes. It was deeply
satisfying and it passed the time.

Then I discovered that, backed up against the wardrobe door, the vibrating arse of the guitar combined with the booming wooden acoustic to create an actual sound. It was still entirely unmusical but it was a small start and, suddenly slightly audible, we baptised ourselves Furniture. Not only was this the title of a very long Horslips song that we would never be able to play, but it was also an in-joke about the wardrobe which only our fans would ever get.

Six months later, however, and fans were still not an issue. Furniture was still unhearable and only when Spit finally bought a second-hand electric amp for himself had we any chance of creating an actual noise of our own. Immediately, we disbanded Furniture and started a new venture called Parabola. It was probably some kind of avant-garde jazz-rock thing although, as ever, we would not have known it at the time.

In the end, however, our severe musical limitations finally drove us headlong into the pit of heavy metal and Parabola soon became Rivet. We realised that we could play Black Sabbath's 'Paranoid' and Deep Purple's 'Smoke on the Water' (apart from the drums, the vocals and the guitar solos) and it made us feel very good indeed. Yes, we sounded like acne but it suited our condition and our mood – scything our mute guitars through the air and imagining ourselves as confident other beings with flowing manes of curly hair. And so began the dreadful and shameful heavy metal years.

It was, of course, an affectation. The important

thing was simply to belong – to join a tribe of any sort and heavy metal, for all its needlework and white basketball boots, promised some kind of fraternity. It also suggested the availability of countless women with big hair and latex legs and this was clearly something which would amount to a major improvement in our circumstances.

And it was all so easy too. To become a rocker, even a pretend one, all you had to do was buy some AC/DC badges in Bus Stop on Belmore Street and get yourself a Motörhead album. That would have been more than enough but then Spit really got into it and started listening to Def Leppard, Gillan, Saxon and Iron Maiden. He made devil's horn signs at anything that moved and he educated himself further by reading *Kerrang!* and *Sounds*. Before long he was reproducing the names of hundreds of bands all over his school books – especially the umlauted Motörhead which he had proudly perfected in full Teutonic script.

They play so loud your ears bleed! he told me in awe. And they have an aeroplane on the stage and Lemmy has no teeth!

Who's Lemmy? I asked.

He's the singer! chided Spit. He can't sing a fuckin' note and his father is a Protestant minister.

So I played along with it – even feigning pleasure in an Australian band called Rose Tattoo who played before Lizzy and U2 at Slane in 1981. Somebody said their lead singer – Angry Anderson – had filed his teeth to sharp points and that was apparently a cool thing to have done. *The Friday Rockshow* on BBC Radio 1 took care of previously desolate weekends and the thunderous Tommy Vance kept us abreast of all the heavy news and more. He played groups like Rush and the Enid and I always dozed off to the last hour of it – my brain tumbling into nightmare vortexes of guitar solos and pot-bellied drummers with far too many drums.

Soon we had learned how to dress the part properly. Sleeveless shirts with rising Japanese suns across our birdcage chests, tight Shakespearean jeans, AC/DC badges, fingerless gloves and hair as long as the school would allow, which was to the collar and no more.

But fortunately Rivet couldn't last. We didn't have a singer or a drummer and so we never actually played anywhere. It was therefore inevitable that we would split – a tough time though when the moment came. Spit decided to go solo and I just stayed at home in my room solemnly jumping around to 'The Boys are Back in Town' or, more often than not, falling asleep again while listening to a Rush double live album called *Exit Stage Left*.

HERO

'Bonsoir, à tout à l'heure, sayanora, farewell, bon voyage,
auf Weidersehen, slán agus beannacht . . . and all the rest
are dirty.'

Phil Lynott

In the summer of 1981, myself and Spit are hovering
in the Dublin sunshine on the lookout for Phil
Lynott. We have no information. We are simply
speculating that he might well be somewhere around
Grafton Street. This is his home town after all and
Thin Lizzy are playing the next day at the first ever
festival at Slane Castle.

He is bound to be somewhere and sure enough, as
we walk though the thick coffee smell of Duke
Street, we suddenly spot him – the only black man
in Ireland, standing outside the Bailey, and looking
more like a star than anything we could ever
imagine.

Holy fuck! blurts Spit.

Cool it, I mutter sideways.

Holy fuck! blurts Spit again.

And so we stand transfixed as Lynott lights a
cigarette, pulls up the collar of a long, long overcoat
and suddenly begins striding towards us – a loping
gait, a dip in his hip, a glide in his stride and his

black, black face deep in a cloud of jet Afro and smoke.

Howya, lads, he smiles as he clocks us clocking him.

Well, Phil, how the fuck are you? says Spit.

Great, howya? says Philip Lynott, staggering to a stop and pointing at our two Thin Lizzy T-shirts. Yiz going to the gig?

Fuck, aye, says Spit.

Whereya from? says Phil Lynott.

Enniskillen.

Did we play there?

Fuckin' right you did, says Spit.

Well, if yiz wanna come around after the show and say hello . . .

And then he pats me on the arm, nods at Spit and walks off – crowds parting in front of him – his huge head of hair disappearing across Grafton Street.

Holy fuck! blurts Spit.

Nobody will believe us, I said.

Philip Parris Lynott was a black Irishman and as cool as it got. He had a dog called Gnasher. He was good to his mother and his granny and he was into football. Teenage girls loved him. Teenage boys wanted to be like him. He mixed the imagery of cowboy, comic-book hero, gigolo, rake, romantic, hard man and old softie, and I wanted to be all of those things – depending on the company.

He had style, charm and power. He threw shapes and he had a face that was easy to capture on the backs of jotters and school books – the bush of hair pulled down over one still visible eye, the thin moustache, the pirate's earring and that one dark eye looking very mean indeed. He read poetry. He wrote poetry. And best of all, and even though he seemed like he had landed from some other world, he was a Dub from Leighlin Road in Crumlin and he made Dublin seem like the hippest place on earth.

The mirror ball had showered stars around the complex as the coyote called and the howling winds wailed. The sirens and the police lights during 'Jailbreak' had taken the eyes out of our heads and the spotlight reflecting off Lynott's bass had picked us out one by one in what felt like a ritual rescue. It had all the wild euphoria of being born again and my excitement had been total, unselfconscious and overwhelming. I could still remember every detail, every incident, every chord and every word. It ran like some incredible movie in my head.

And now we had met him. In person and in the flesh. What we did not know was that Philip Lynott was on drugs in a very serious way. That when Thin Lizzy came to Enniskillen in 1980, he had a bad habit; and that when we went to see him play at Slane Castle the following summer, he had a very bad habit. Of course, we could not have known it at the time and, in any case, we would not have believed it anyway because Philo was the leader of our wild but entirely benign gang.

We had always kind of hoped that Phil would be just like us – not doing anything really bad – just swaggering a bit and acting the lad. But all those times we travelled to see Thin Lizzy, he was completely messed up on heroin and booze and soon the person I most wanted to be like in the whole world would be dead and buried in Howth.

I knew nothing about drugs. Spit knew nothing about them either apart from his messy attempts to smoke dried banana skins and, on one occasion, a plastic bagful of dulse. So the death of Phil Lynott in January 1986 was all a huge and angry shock. Our only previous exposure was the time when someone called Billy Chemicals came to the school to warn us of the danger and told us how he had wasted his youth taking every drug he could get his hands on – impressing upon us the foolishness of throwing away our lives partying.

Some fuckin' chance of that! groaned Spit.

In fact, it seemed that people were always warning us about things that were never available in the first place. Our mothers seemed to think that every night we went out, we would somehow be seduced by bad women who would spike our lemonades and take us to their fleshy beds and now here we had Billy Chemicals worried about us getting hooked on cocaine – presumably as we toyed with lines of spilled salt on the pastel-coloured tables of the school dinner hall.

And so the Billy Chemicals project failed completely. Insisting that he had misspent his youth hanging around with Keith Moon and Jimi Hendrix was hardly a convincing argument for a bunch of quite desperate teenagers. In fact, to us, it seemed that Billy Chemicals had led a truly marvellous life. If only we could be like Billy Chemicals, because he was, by far, the most exotic thing to have appeared at St Gavin's since the bishop's brand-new hat.

DISCO INFERNO

'We find birdsong charming and attractive but of course,
mostly, that's just the sound of "Come here so I can shag
you!" or "Get off my fucking territory!" Those are
basically the two messages that are coming out. I don't
think, mostly, that they're singing for joy.'

Brian Eno

School discos were the jittery events which served as
our first legitimate teenage occasions. They happened once a month amid extraordinary tension and
speculation – all of it confused and misdirected.
Precisely what we hoped to achieve by them is
another teenage imponderable but there was something genuinely dislocating about them and the way
the gloomy corridors of St Gavin's were transformed
into something almost exciting and vaguely glam.

Surely this could not be the same stale place of
earlier in the day? The place where we gripped the
clanking radiators to get the frost out of our hands
and the rain out of our trouser legs? Surely these
could not be the same corridors which by day were
governed by dry and distant dogma, but were now
run by the giddy chaotic laws of sex and perfumed
hair – girls soaked in Anaïs Anaïs and promising the
pressured warmth of a slow dance? Surely some

mistake? Surely some rip in the space–time continuum?

Shay Love would always be the first on the floor. He would leap out under the lights like a shocked octopus and begin. His arms would flail and his eyes, like a chameleon's, would pop and roll in all directions at once as a circle of stunned space widened out around him.

I am the God of Hellfire! he would shout. Gabba Gabba Hey! Timid country girls would shelter behind each other as Shay would collapse to his knees in deep and determined prayer before springing into some frantic locked in a box, trapped in a bubble, shooting heroin and hanging himself mime. The Dean of Studies would look briefly concerned but then would just sigh, shake his head and evaporate.

And then when Shay Love had finally collapsed in exhaustion and had crawled out into the night air, it would be time for the girls to activate themselves as best they could and slowly move towards the centre of the dance floor – two steps forward and one step back. It was always a deflating sight, all false promise suddenly gone as they huddled in their tight groups and transformed into many-headed things that bobbed, swayed and excluded all intruders.

And yet they would keep looking over their shoulders to see if anybody was looking at them, and of course nobody ever did. Only the really determined ever bothered to pay them any attention at all. The rest of us just pretended to be bored, which wasn't difficult given that we really were bored. But we would act out our parts even so, sulkily aware that this disco ritual, however pointless, would simply have to be endured.

Do you like Horslips? Floyd McAloon would eventually ask some red-faced redhead from Boho.

I do, she would say. Do you like Horslips?

I do surely, he would smile, but have you ever seen them?

Naw, but me brother seen them in the Astoria Ballroom. Have you seen them?

It has a bouncy floor so it has, Floyd would add with a confident grin.

What has?

The Astoria Ballroom. In Bundoran. Do you have any of their records?

I have all of them except for 'Happy to Meet Sorry to Part', she would say.

I'll maybe lend it to you, Floyd would say. It's shaped like a concertina.

What is?

The record sleeve.

Oh?

Aye, you should see it, Floyd would say, it's class.

And soon they would be shouting eagerly in each other's ears. She would be animated, smiling, touching his shoulder as she spoke. He would then be away in a hack and so, on his coat-tails, I would corner her greasy friend.

Do *you* like Horslips? I would ask.

Naw, she would reply, looking uneasily at her

red-faced, red-headed friend. And then I would change tack.

Do you like Thin Lizzy?

Naw, she would say, this time looking at the ceiling.

Well, then, do you like Rory Gallagher? I would ask.

Naw, she would answer finally and firmly and I would mutter some face-saving insult under my breath and return to the corner where we would all resume pushing each other about and pretending to laugh out loud.

No joy? Spit would jeer, poking me in the chest.

They really know nothing at all about music! I would bark.

Who?

Women! I would growl. They know bugger all!

And for a time, most of us really began to believe that girls just couldn't hear music properly. After all, they bought all the wrong singles and it almost seemed wilful. Anything we thought was uncool and embarrassing, they would profess to love. And any singer who was obviously a tube, they would have his picture stuck on the back of their school books. It seemed like just another female mystery that we couldn't be bothered to solve.

But we did know that there were girls out there somewhere, in Dublin probably, who must have liked Thin Lizzy. Why else would there be pin-ups of Phil Lynott in *Jackie*? But at our school discos it was all Duran Duran and Spandau Ballet and so all we could do was wait impatiently for the whole quiffy charade to end, hurry to that stage of the night where we would yield once again to the tyrannies of attraction and count ourselves out. We would never, we reminded ourselves, be doing anything legal or illegal, moral or immoral, pure or impure, modest or immodest with anybody of the opposite sex at a school disco in Fermanagh. It just wasn't on.

Nobody really cared that much anyway. We didn't really fancy anybody out there on the floor of the dining hall, because while we were very innocent, we were not entirely stupid. We had seen the pictures – American women with curves and curvettes and big, big hair and nobody at these school discos seemed to belong to even the same species. It seemed that, as usual, we would all just have to wait until we got to the States. In the meantime, however, all we could do was display just how little we really cared with one of our male-only headbanging sessions. And in the grotesque process we could put the pointless night out of its thumping misery.

And so we would form a circle and shake our heads to the zigzagging chords of 'A Whole Lotta Rosie' or the slow build of 'Freebird' as our fingers hit every note on every imaginary guitar. Our backs would sweat, our shirts would cling, our aftershave would reek, our necks would ache, our spots would itch, our brains would spin and keep spinning until that moment when our desperate hearts would have to sink once more – the last slow song of the night drifting on to the floor to really finish us off and rub it in.

It was a smuggled copy of 'Je t'aime' and all it did was taunt us further with that other world in which we all wanted to live – a foreign place full of erotic sounds and silk sheets. And then when the two French voices had eventually finished making their deep French love – something we couldn't even imagine – the lights would flicker on and the cold frustrating school would become the cold frustrating school once more.

We were paler now, drained and spottier than ever, sweaty and wasted, defeated and full of some familiar anger. And then as the girls began to grab their coats and each other, everyone would flow out into the freezing night in a confused river of hormones and silence. Cold sweat. Cold hearts. And the long empty walk home.

But then there was the night that Spit scored and headed in another direction entirely. Somebody he'd encountered needed walking home and he was the very impatient man to do it.

You must be mad, I whispered in horror as I surveyed his conquest from across the floor.

Fuck off! he snapped.

Next day he told me all about it and I knew, by the way of him, that everything had changed for ever. It was sad. He stopped spitting, he stopped swearing, he stopped listening to music and I immediately suspected that he was under strong pressure to stop hanging around with me. And I was right. Quite suddenly my best friend vanished from my life altogether and all I could do was scoff bitterly as he went off on his long solemn walks with his big-legged girlfriend – his thumb hooked in the back pocket of her jeans, and hers in his. They were a sorry and unconvincing sight but, for them, the achievement and the confirmation was all.

INSPIRATION INFORMATION

'It was in Dallas, Texas, and there was no television, there was no telephone, there was no Coke machine, there was no swimming pool – there was nothing – and I just sat there for three days. And then I felt this song just drift through the window.'

Townes Van Zandt

Zeus and Mnemosyne had nine daughters with very swanky names – Urania, Thalia, Clio, Calliope, Melpomene, Erato, Polyhymnia, Euterpe and Terpsichore. They were known as the Muses and, unlike any girls I had ever met, they were beautiful, sophisticated and half naked. All they did was lie languidly on mountainsides, plucking flowers, dancing, strumming and inspiring men to great works of art.

And while they were goddesses of all intellectual pursuits, it was really only four of them who had any real bearing on my life during the short wet summer of 1982 – the year I was asked to join Shay Love's band, the Children of Prague. The foursome in question were: Erato, who looked after lyric poetry and the lyre; Euterpe, the flute maiden; Polyhymnia, whose speciality was singing to the gods; and Terpsichore, the all-singing all-dancing entertainer who had clearly devoted as much time to Shay Love as he had to her.

The Greeks, he once told Radio North, did not invent music (he kept saying *mousike*) but they certainly paid more attention to it than, say, the Romans or the showbands. Don't forget, he went on, that the Greeks invented the scales and just because we choose to ignore them does not necessarily mean that we don't know them when we see them. The crucial thing, however, and what I'm really trying to say, is that the Children of Prague are an art movement and the leading voices of the Fermanagh Renaissance . . .

Yes indeed, humphed the fat and ancient interviewer full of smug provincial contempt, I understand that you are from *Fermanagh*.

He said the word like they were the most loathsome three syllables imaginable.

We are indeed, said Shay, brightly ignoring the tone, and at the same time, we are not. We are creatures of music. You might be one yourself if you weren't a golfer. I think you look like a man who plays a lot of golf. Plato never played golf because he was too busy using his brain.

Is that Plato or Pluto? sneered the radio man, giggling at his own joke.

Plato, Pluto, Bono, Ono and Eno, whispered Shay Love ominously. And whatever you're having yourself – I'll hold out two shovels and you can take your pick. But Plato, the man I'm talking about, believed that music went beyond its immediate effect to mould the character of the listener. And he also said that you cannot be a true musician unless you understand temperance, fortitude, liberality and magnificence. No mention of golf anywhere there, is there?

And you have all those things, do you? hissed the interviewer.

Yes indeed, said Shay Love with conviction, it's what sets the Children of Prague apart from the rest – from the pop scene, from the golf scene and, most of all, from the grotesque excesses of the Showband Era. I'm going out on a limb here but you were probably in a showband yourself? You have that look about you.

No, I wasn't actually, said the cocksure interviewer, but I have been known to . . .

At least they played their own instruments, eh? interrupted Shay, all them crappy showbands, eh?

Well, thank you very much, fussed the interviewer, bringing the conversation to a sudden end. That was Shay Love of the group the Prague Children [sic] destined, they tell me, for the top of the hit parade . . . anyway here's an old favourite from the New Seekers for Betty in Hillsborough who is ninety-three years young today. This comes from all the family and from all her friends in the Omega Old People's Home . . .

At that point Shay Love was distinctly heard to mutter, Oh, for fuck's sake . . .

There then followed a long three-second silence and the New Seekers came on to try to make everything alright again. But the anaesthetic did not have the desired effect and soon there were predictable complaints made to the station – irate housewives, clergymen, cranky old bastards, golfers and several showband veterans who thought that Shay Love was an appalling barbarian and that young people today were dreadful. On the positive side, there was one curious call from a 'fascinated' academic from the University of Ulster and no less than seventeen calls of support all made from the same public phone box in Enniskillen.

It was a typical Children of Prague stunt. All we were ever after was reaction and we got it without fail. Basically, although we were not aware of it, we were a performance-art group. In fact, there was nobody quite like us, except perhaps for the Virgin Prunes who operated out of Dublin. The difference was that they knew what they were doing because they had read books and, while they were still at school, they had gone on the boat to see Bowie.

We on the other hand were totally ignorant chancers and that was our charm. In a way, that made us far better than them and they knew it too. There was once an extraordinary bust-up between us in a tiny studio at RTE after which both bands were unofficially barred from any further television appearances. Even the tapes were erased in an attempt to write both our musics out of the official history of Irish rock.

But the music of the Children really was groundbreaking, outsider stuff and, despite the censorship, it had its unique influence even so. It was mostly unrepeatable and mucksavage – an inexplicable improvisation which left audiences bewildered, beaten and upset. Original, powerful and unforgettable, the Children of Prague were indisputably Fermanaghs' greatest band.

This is not a rebel song! Shay Love once screamed at a Sunday lunchtime audience at the Alcock and Brown Hotel in Clifden, County Galway. This is not a song of any description! So lay down your knives and your forks and get a load of this. This is the way we do it in the Erne Basin!

And then he sang 'The Holy Ground', 'New Year's Day', 'Telegram Sam', 'Oliver's Army' and 'Arthur McBride', all rolled together in voices that shifted from croon to growls to falsetto to shouts to screams and wails. The audience, which had innocently stopped in after Mass, tried at first to concentrate on their lunches, stabbing angrily at their scampi and cursing the racket under their breaths. But we knew that they could not ignore us for ever and sure enough, before very long, they had put down their cutlery and were just staring up at us open-mouthed like a nestful of helpless scaldies waiting to be fed.

Shay worked the room with confounding energy and neck, and led us through our totally improvised set – we were, after all, a band with no compunction, no compromise and, above all, no actual repertoire. As with every other gig, we somehow created an explosive, cacophonous nothingness which we managed to sustain for an hour and fifteen minutes. It wasn't easy but we did it and not a single person finished their lunch. It was therefore a total victory.

We are Dada! Shay kept shouting. Dada! Dada! Dada! Dada! Dada! Dada! Dada! Dada! Dada! Dada! Dada! Dada! Dada! Dada! Dada! Dada!!

'No we were never Dada,' Shay Love said ten years later in a nostalgic *Hot Press* piece on Northern rock. 'In fact, we were not anything that I can think of. Some bands can say that what you saw was what you got, but we cannot really say that. Most of the time the Children were not what you got. What you saw was *not* what you got. But having said that, we were without question the best band to have ever crawled out of Lough Erne and the greatest thing to happen in County Fermanagh since Tom Thumb turned up on the Main Street in 1871.'

THE BROTHERS

'They took me out of school in 1944 and sent me right into the hands of the Japs. I got wounded a couple of times, I got my head blown open by a hand grenade, I was in a prisoner-of-war camp for eighteen months and then when I came out of that, I was caught right up in the Korean War. I played crazy, tried to go home and I succeeded. That took years out of my life because I spent three years in a mental institution and I never know today if there's sanity in me or insanity. I don't know if I'm right or if I'm wrong – I only know that to be nice, to laugh and to smile is a rare commodity and I try to do all I can in that department. But at the same time, when I think of all the things that happened to me, I should either be dead by now or just wasting away in some institution. How I survived all of that, only God's got the answer.'

Screamin' Jay Hawkins

Because Ignatius, formerly known as Spit, formerly known as my best friend, was now the property of his big-legged woman and I was a Child of Prague with few fantasies left of trying to be a serious rock star, I began to spend more and more time with the meditative and eccentric Bart – second cousin of John Lennon and inventor of his own language.

John Lennon may be my cousin or he may not, he would say, but I do know that he is a Brother and in a world of future hens that is more important than anything your granny says about the price of coal. There's no future for a future hen when the horse is staring into the mouth of the field with a long face on him, etc., etc.

But quite desperate for company and any fanciful flight out of Fermanagh, I determined to tune into Bart and, before long, I was able to converse with him in a fairly basic way.

Brother Maguire, how's your nose today?

Very well, Brother Lydon, the right nostril is currently flaring better than the left.

For him to call me Brother was a huge benediction. It meant that he respected me and that I was now part of his extremely exclusive Angel Soul Brotherhood – a gathering of talent brought together to provide comfort for his isolated self. Membership included Van Morrison, Bob Dylan, John Keats, William Wordsworth, James Joyce, Tom Waits, Mozart, Van Gogh, Magritte, Flann O'Brien, Yeats, Gerard Manley Hopkins, Coleridge, Beckett, Rimbaud, and so on. None of them knew of their membership but Bart needed them around him even so.

These are the Brothers, he announced, pointing to a collage of extraordinary faces on his bedroom door. They *know* and I *know*. I asked about the ones I recognised.

Why Beckett? I asked.

Because, Brother Declan, of the following exchange. A French interviewer asks him, *Monsieur*

Beckett, vous êtes anglais? And Brother Beckett replies, *Au contraire*. What about that for an answer? A class response, wasn't it? He went to school in Enniskillen, you know. A good swimmer too.

A face like the Hanging Rock, I said.

A precipice, agreed Bart.

And why Flann O'Brien? We're doing him in Irish.

Atomic theory, said Bart knowingly.

And who is that?

Wordsworth, said Bart with a gracious smile.

And why him?

The Prelude. The bit in the boat.

Oh, and Bob Dylan? I said lighting up. He's a Brother alright.

Oh yes, anybody who can rhyme *vandals* and *handles*.

So how come you address me as Brother? I asked with some humility.

Because you *are* a Brother, said Bart.

But I've never done anything, I said feebly.

Ah, said Bart, but you understand the whole nose project.

Of course I did not understand anything about the nose project. In fact, I wasn't even aware that there *was* a whole nose project, but I nodded very gratefully anyway. As a member of Bart Maguire's Angel Soul Brotherhood, I could now, in some way, be connected up with that giant bicycle wheel of a universe, the centre of which was the mad collage on

Bart's bedroom door. And although no other Brothers, apart from ourselves, knew that the Brotherhood even existed, it somehow made us all colleagues and co-conspirators against the void. Most importantly of all, it raised levels of possibility, ambition and hope.

There's no doubt that we needed to associate, even in our own tiny minds, with people who had, in their own way, escaped their own personal Fermanagh. We did not for a minute think that we were equal partners with, for example, James Joyce and Bob Dylan, but there was certainly a huge satisfaction in their actual presence.

And so we began to live in our own enormous but private cosmos, unrestricted by time, space, life or death. It was a place where Yeats could meet Bart and Bart could meet Leonard Cohen and then Bart could introduce him to Yeats and we could write a song for them and Beckett could sing it – maybe backwards. It passed the time. And it dug a ridiculous but feasible tunnel to the here and now.

And then one night in Bart's room as I sipped from a tumbler of diluted orange which hadn't been diluted enough, he deftly tilted a record from its sleeve, held its edges with the palms of his hands, angled its spectrums to the light, blew on it silently and gently placed it on the foamy turntable. I waited as the needle clunked, amplified and expectantly hissed into life.

This, said Bart with extraordinary reverence, is Van Morrison. This song is called 'Listen to the

Lion'. And now I would like us to listen to Brother Van.

And so we listened to the growls and the whispers and suddenly, out of nowhere, here was a music that I understood completely. As it moved like some comforting warm river through my brain, it was as if I was singing it myself. I knew it already. I understood it and yet it was shocking to me – like something which had always been living, crankily, inside me and was now, at last, able to come joyfully out.

Brother Bart, I gushed when the song had ended, who the flip is Van Morrissey?

His name is Morrison. He is from Belfast. He lives in America but many years ago he was in Derrygonnelly. I know that for a fact.

HIGHWAY 61

'The purpose of music is to make people feel good, to make people feel love. It gives people a spiritual love – a love feeling.'

Brian Wilson

It was a cool, orangey-pink summer's morning when Shay Love, Bart Maguire and myself stepped out into the dewy ditch and stuck out our three adventurous thumbs. We were off to Slane Castle to see Bob Dylan and, for the very first time in our lives, we were truly conscious that we were going somewhere worth going – somewhere vital.

I had first heard of Bob Dylan when a neighbour named his son after him – something unheard of in those days. Enniskillen was, after all, a place where even my own name Declan was considered a bit fancy Dan. What was even more bizarre about this Dylan baptism is that, instead of being called after some reliable Irish saint, the baby was being named for some folk singer who sang through his nose – some kind of hippie who could sing none. The fact that guitar-toting plain-clothes nuns liked to sing 'Blowin' in the Wind' was neither here nor there.

But as soon as I heard Dylan for myself I was away. I jumped straight in and, through steady listening, I unconsciously learned the words to almost every song. It was, according to Brother Bart, something called Spiritual Osmosis and, before long, I was living inside these extraordinary lyrics. I couldn't have been more ready for Slane and Bob Dylan – just to witness the man, to bear witness to the work. And so out with the three thumbs – thumb one, thumb two, thumb three.

After tramping about a mile and a half and just beginning to get a little panicky, a long sleek silvery car whooshed past out of nowhere. Suddenly, it skidded to a lumpy stop and we looked at each other and grinned slyly. Then instantly withdrawing the three thumbs we sprinted, all smiles, to the descending steamy window.

Thanks very much, mister, I said.

And then I got a serious drop. This wasn't a mister at all, this was a father and the dawn driver of this silver machine was Father Tiernach Loughran – a former teacher at St Gavin's, now a curate in the sticks and someone we admired about as much as we did Seamie Sheridan and his Shite Shamrock Showband. His nickname was Starsky and he was the maddest driver in the country. Every time he went down that avenue from St Gavin's, schoolboys had to dive into the sheugh.

We looked at each other horrified. We'd never get there. He'd kill us all in some gruesome pile-up before we even got over the border. And worse again, this was not the way to begin our first Jack Kerouac adventure on the road – the plan having been to hitch a lift with three loose hippie women in a van full of drugs and mattresses. But because Slane Castle and Bob Dylan were still several counties away, we silently agreed that a lift was a lift. In any case, he would only be going as far as Monaghan which was the place where all priests came from and returned to whenever they got the chance. And so, grimly, we dunted each other into the back seat and tried to behave.

You'll have to remind me of your names again, boys, he said with half a smile.

Shay Love, said Shay.

Did I ever teach you, Shay?

Yes, Father, you did.

What did I teach you?

Not a whole lot, Father.

I elbowed Shay sharply in the ribs but somehow Starsky was still engaging with the answer to his first question and didn't seem to have heard.

Love, you say. Are you from the town?

Yes, Father. I'm not some kind of culchie, if that's what you mean.

And who else have we here?

Bart Maguire, said Bart.

And Declan Lydon, I said.

Maguire and Lydon? he whispered as he tried to locate us in his head. Are you both from the town?

We are, said Bart, we are all loving angels in a world of contraception.

Starsky was lost in thought.

Sorry, what's that you say?

Nothing, Father, I said.

As he quickly accelerated to a steady eighty-five, I began to pray that he would start concentrating on the bends of the unapproved road instead of constantly eyeing us suspiciously in the mirror – the three of us tightly squeezed together in the back seat and beginning to sweat with the furious speed and the screeching bends.

So you are off to see Bob Dylan then, boys?

Aye.

Aye.

Aye.

Well, you're in luck, boys, because that's where I'm going myself. Isn't that great! We can all go together!

Sweet fuck! mouthed Shay Love in silent panic.

This was a serious situation. We were hardly going to pick up at least three women between here and Slane in a car driven by a priest who was also a teacher. If anybody saw us we'd be finished and we knew we had to get out of this. We knew we had to lose the priest, but do we lose him now or do we wait until we get to Slane?

We conferred frantically with our eyes. We muttered, we whispered, we made hand signals and we seemed to agreed that we would worry about it once we got there. OK, there would be no adventures on the road with sex-crazed hippies or drugged-up rock chicks – but at least we would get to the gig. And that was the main thing after all.

Oh, Bob Dylan's just marvellous! offered Starsky merrily. *The vandals took the handles!* I love that!

Bart began to choke. Up until that moment, the only teacher who ever seemed to know anything about anything interesting was an art teacher who had shown us photographs of David Bowie as Ziggy Stardust. He had taken them himself with a long lens at a concert somewhere in England – Ziggy all angles, bones, woolly stockings and make-up. Of course, being us – the disconnected – we didn't really know who David Bowie was and we were far more impressed by the fact that he had taken the photographs without permission. In any case, a shaken Spit quickly advised us that Ziggy Stardust looked very like a fruit to him.

But now here was a teacher (and a priest) who was into Bob Dylan. The whole thing was unthinkable and the whole disruption of it began to cause overload in the back seat. We were so easily rattled by anything which challenged our dull certainties and this time we were so rattled that we were sick.

When we finally entered the outskirts of Slane, after what seemed like a very long and sweaty silence, the three of us kept our heads well down. We just could not afford to be seen in the back of Starsky's car – two members of the Children of Prague (one of them formerly of Hot Vomit) and two members of the Angel Soul Brotherhood including the Grand Brother himself. It was a potential apocalypse.

Keep your heads down! ordered Shay. I'll think of something.

And then, hours later, when we reckoned that Starsky had finally reversed his car to a stop on what felt like a humpy field of unmarked graves, we looked at each other in our dark huddle and held our breaths as Shay whispered backwards from three to one.

Now! he roared. Go, go, go!

And so we burst out of the car as if it were a landing craft on a beachhead — myself and Bart diving low to our left, falling twice and crashing into a Hare Krishna stall. Shay had to clamber back over the bonnet of the car and follow us, rolling and tumbling, into the crowd — an earthquake pathway of fear clearing in front of him. Meanwhile, as we vanished into eighty thousand sunburned torsos, back in his silver car the Reverend Father Starsky was probably wondering what he had done wrong.

There was only the slightest nip of guilt, however, and when Bob Dylan appeared our whole world blew up. I had never experienced an excitement like it as when I first laid eyes on him — taking the stage as if he had just walked into the wrong room. There seemed to be some sense of accident about the whole thing. Here he was on the Banks of the Boyne — the setting for Nigel Johnston's only song — and he looked both startled and stern, covered in orange make-up with thick black eyeliner and a dangling earring quivering by his cheek. He squinted down at the thousands, his eyebrows raised like two big question marks as he bounced back and forth on his heels. And then, after taking one more look at the front rows and picking out the three of us, he shrugged and turned to the band.

C'mon, Brother Bob! shouted Bart. Give it the welly!

And so we watched as Bob Dylan dug his fingers into his temples, shook his head as if to clear it, and broke into 'Highway 61'. It was my very first contact with someone whose voice I had lived with for so long. And then at the very end, who marches on – only Van Morrison to duet on 'It's All Over Now, Baby Blue' and 'Tupelo Honey'! If the three of us – Bart Maguire, Shay Love and Declan Lydon – had been assumed into heaven at that particular moment, we could not have been happier. But how we actually got there in the first place was never mentioned again.

BIRDCAGE OF THE MUSES

'Until I joined Mick and Keith and Brian I didn't know anything about the blues. That's when I first heard Jimmy Reed, Elmore James, Muddy Waters and Bo Diddley. It was all pretty new to me. Me, Charlie and Ian Stewart used to jump in a taxi and go to the black areas of Chicago or Atlanta and we'd stop at the first record shop we could find. We'd jump out, run in, grab handfuls of singles and albums, pay for them really quickly and rush back to the hotel. You'd come up with gems like Lazy Lester or Lonesome Sundown and then you'd record them.'

Bill Wyman

The most important place in town was the new library. Much as I had once discovered sweets at the Pick 'n' Mix section of Wellworths, I could go in there every Saturday morning, gaze in bewilderment at the heavy rolling waves of records stuffed into the racks, and then make my determined choices. Between Shay, Bart and myself, we took out nine albums a week and circulated them in a well-organised criss-cross of permutations and home taping. Home taping was killing music, but not for us.

The biggest well of wisdom was the back catalogue of Van Morrison who became the most crucial touchstone. He constantly name-checked other singers or sang songs by other musicians with yet stranger names: Leadbelly, Blind Lemon, Sonny Terry and Brownie McGhee, Jimmie Rodgers, Muddy Waters, Jackie Wilson, Hank Williams, Sonny Boy Williamson and Bobby Bland. The Stones and Rory Gallagher were other valuable sources and soon we were pulling out records by all these brand-new people who lurked undisturbed in the packed racks of the library.

Full of excitement, we would take them home to our unsuspecting houses, settle them on the stereo and wait for delicious shock after shock. And almost always we were propelled further into a state of surprise and delight. Who were all these people? Why had we never heard of them? And why was it all so much better than anything we had ever heard before?

What is *that*? shouted Shay up at my open window on The Long Road.

Howlin' Wolf! I shouted down.

Harland and Wolff? They built the *Titanic*.

Howlin' Wolf! I corrected. Chester Burnett!

Shit! screamed Shay, his eyes popping out. That's unbelievable! We might as well just fuck everything else in the bin!

It was as if we had found and opened a boarded-up door into a place that nobody even knew existed. And our investigations led us in all directions – Chuck Berry, Freddy King, Elmore James, Louisiana

Red, Jimmy Reed, B.B. King, Albert King, Lightnin' Hopkins, Bo Diddley, Buddy Guy, Willie Dixon, Otis Rush, Lazy Lester, Lonesome Sundown, Slim Harpo and Champion Jack all rolled in. Then older stuff again – Blind Willie McTell, the Memphis Jug Band, Charley Patton, Robert Johnson, Son House, the Mississippi Sheiks, Bo Carter, Scrapper Blackwell, Leroy Carr, Blind Willie Johnson and Skip James all crackled out of another time and ghosted into my bedroom. Theirs was a music so intimate that I could smell the gin on their breaths, the smoke on their pinstripe suits and see tiny red veins make maps of the Delta in their heavy, clouded eyes.

You're wasting your time! Shay complained forcefully to a bunch of younger library cardholders who were innocently looking for pop. Take these out and listen to them or I'll beat the crap out of yis!

And then shoving albums by Papa George Lightfoot and Memphis Slim into the trembling arms of the innocents, he smiled like a mad saint or a spirit guide.

But what is it? one of young ones asked.

It's *real* music! Just listen to it or I'll bloody well kill you! And don't be taking out any more music by white people! It's all shite!

Next thing, Bart took up the harmonica and began to bend notes every chance he got. He started out by practising on one owned by Hugthebottle – a local fixture who would vamp through his bloodied hands as he staggered home as full as a bingo bus every day in life. But Hugthebottle's harmonica, full of boozy fumes, was not the right kind for playing dirty blues and Bart soon stopped pestering him for the loan of it. He needed a Marine Band Blues harp in the key of A, and when he finally got one sent down from a cousin in Dublin, he very quickly learned to play almost properly – Bart wailing in A as Shay hammered his guitar in E.

It's cross-harp, said Bart, real low-down. Like Sonny Boy II – Rice Miller – not Sonny Boy Williamson I, who was a different man altogether. He's the one who did 'Baby Please Don't Go' that Them did. Sonny Boy Williamson II does 'Help Me' and 'Take Your Hand Out of My Pocket' – you know the songs Van does on the live album with the Caledonia Soul Orchestra?

Gutbucket! agreed Spit. Chitlin circuit!

Soon the two of them had transformed the Erne into the muddy Mississippi flowing all the way to Ballyshannon through the cottonfields of Fermanagh and the fertile cornpatches of Donegal. And all that freakish warm July we sat, night after night, in clouds of vicious midgies and tormented the German tourists with our late-night blues jams – endless twelve-bars in the raunchy key of E.

This is Fermanagh music, Bart spoofed to an eager family from München with an umlaut, this music was invented here. Blind Francie Maguire was a one-legged poitín maker from Belcoo and he started it. Don't believe what you read in the books because

Blind Francie was my great-great-grandfather and he's the man. And when you think about it, he's the very man who invented rock 'n' roll. Elvis Presley my arse! 'That's Alright Mama' – he wrote that.

And soon the Germans were clapping along and feeding us beer and cheese. And Bart improvised his lyrics about the Killyhevlin Hotel and why we hated going to the discos there and he made *Fermanagh* rhyme with *Mama* and got as lewd as his limited understanding would allow. And then as the jetty rocked to the thump of sixteen feet – eight of them in Adidas trainers, the rest in exotic yellow wellies – we were as happy and free as we could possibly have been without actually heading down the real Mississippi and away.

Before long, Belcoo was Clarksdale, Irvinestown was Greenville, Lisnaskea was Vicksburg, Derrygonnelly was Indianola, Tempo was Yazoo City and Enniskillen was Memphis itself. The Erne no longer ran north to Ballyshannon but south to New Orleans and we lived it as thoroughly as we could for that last long glorious summer.

On one particularly giddy night, we waited, at Bart's insistence, at a crossroads on the Sligo Road in quiet expectation of the Devil himself – a tall man in a black coat with a velvet collar who would appear at midnight, retune Shay's guitar and hand it back. But as the bells of the cathedral sounded through the damp clouds, the only person who appeared out of the soup was a very plastered Hugthebottle – kicking his own dog, playing his harmonica and singing 'He'll Have to Go'.

Also in the library, we found yet another door waiting to be opened. Jazz was something I had heard of (and I knew it to be truly mysterious stuff) but it was a language I could not possibly have known. Doctors in the hospital liked jazz. People in the rugby club seemed to like it too, but the only jazz I had ever heard seemed like comedy music and I didn't like it at all. It always seemed to be played by men in bowler hats and spangly waistcoats and it sounded silly and fake.

But this was different. Here was someone called John Coltrane and he looked very cool indeed. And Miles Davis and Cannonball Adderley and Sonny Rollins. I hadn't heard of any of them and so I settled on Coltrane's *My Favorite Things* and snuck it home for a secret sacred attempt. I stayed in all that weekend, and played the record over and over again, awestruck on my quilt and, lost in this new spectacular music, I was released, entranced and transported.

I stared at the sleeve in its sharp plastic cover and repeated the strange names to myself again and again – McCoy Tyner, Elvin Jones, Nesuhi Ertegun, Phil Iehle, Lee Friedlander, Richard Rodgers and Oscar Hammerstein, DuBose Heyward and George Gershwin, the Atlantic Recording Corporation, 1841 Broadway, New York 23, New York. Yes, I was still in my bedroom, but I wasn't really. I was temporarily gone.

The appeal of it was probably simple enough. It was an improvised music – made on the hoof, as you heard it, and so it was specifically of the moment. In fact, it was so much of the moment that it could never be played in the same way again and I realised that I was hearing an actual thrilling arrangement of the present. Here at last was the actual sound and the actual experience of the here and now. Even in Fermanagh, even on the Long Road, this was the sound of life itself.

What had happened to me, alone with *My Favorite Things*, would have been inexplicable and quite overwhelming if not for the fact that my English teacher had just been explaining, via *Dubliners*, what an epiphany was. And hearing John Coltrane for the very first time, I knew I had just experienced a really big one. Life, I knew, was finally under way, and soon epiphany after epiphany began whooshing in like the screeching squadrons of swifts slicing the evening air in the drizzle of Church Street, Darling Street and Hall's Lane.

GIANT STEPS

'It all had a magnetic effect on me. It was self-expression, and because it was improvised, it kind of pulled me into it in a way that other music never did.'

Herbie Hancock

The reading lamp on the table warmed my cheek as I made my nightly attempts to deal with the looming borderlands of A levels and release. I stared at pages, I underlined, I bracketed, I highlighted and I curled my hair with my fingers until it hurt. Sometimes I skimmed, sometimes I forced, but mostly I just eyeballed the text in anger before putting my head down on the cool of the page to dream my music-driven dreams of other places – New Orleans, Memphis, New York, Chicago and Kansas City.

Every night in life, dozing over *Middlemarch* or 'The Pardoner's Tale', I escaped to all these places and began to make my first real journeys in my head – slipping off, via America and its music, to some external place far from those echoing examination halls which would slam into shocking silences in just a few weeks' time. Yes, I was bitterly stuck in some metered trap of vague industry, but I had little faith left in a system which, so far, had kept all the good stuff so far out of sight.

That said, I did want to go to university – a place where it had been suggested all would somehow be revealed. And, just as importantly, it seemed like the only tunnel out of town. Shay and Bart, however, had other ideas. Shay, who had no notion of further schooling, was dead set on simply hanging around Dublin while Bart announced with great ceremony that he would be off to Tibet the first chance he got. When I asked him where exactly Tibet was, he replied that it didn't matter a damn.

What I really wanted to do was go to New York to hear Miles Davis play the trumpet, but that didn't wash with the teacher temporarily charged with our futures. He had never heard of Miles Davis and just told me I'd better get my act together.

Lydon, he said, this is the real world.

I'm not sure that it is, I muttered.

Catch yourself on, Lydon, he said.

OK then, I said, put me down for teaching. It seems like a cushy number.

C'mon, Lydon! Act your age! What about law?

I don't want to do law, I said.

What if you get the grades for it?

I'll not get the grades for it, I said.

Not the way you're going – you and your heavy metal . . .

I'm into jazz now, I said sullenly.

Oh, jazz is it? Some kind of a beatnik now, are you?

Well, have *you* any bright ideas? I asked half seriously. I mean, I've been at this school for seven

136

years and I still know bugger all about anything. And whose fault is that?

So I'll put you down for law then?

Put me down for any damn thing, I said, any damn thing except the priesthood.

But then things picked up. One night, as I sat stewing, still slumbering over *Middlemarch* and listening to Sonny Rollins at very low volume, my mother called to me up the stairs.

Declan! You're a-wanted!

I'm studying! I shouted back unconvincingly.

You have a visitor! she said and immediately I heard a wild rumble of feet galloping up the stairs. I had never had a visitor in my life and so I was quite terrified at what it might mean. Maybe it was the SAS coming to lift me for listening to Luke Kelly singing 'Kelly the Boy from Killane'? Or, on the bright side, maybe it was some mad beautiful poetess I had never met, coming to tell me that she loved me? Or maybe it was Bob Dylan in town for a meeting of the Brothers? I had no idea but it was scary and I straightened myself up, wiped the drool off my cheek and stared wide-eyed with panic as the bedroom door flung open. No knock.

Well, for fuck's sake, Deccy! You call this work!

It was Spit. I hadn't really spoken to him in over a year – half huffing because he was always too busy taking his bit to the Ritz to see things like *An Officer and a Gentleman* to ever bother calling for me. What

he saw in her I couldn't say, but to hell with him –
him and his *relationship*.

What are you doing here? I asked sulkily.

Just thought I'd call in, he said.

So, *Ignatius* . . .

Don't call me that! he interrupted. My name is
Spit, fuckye.

Oh, so you're Spit again, are you? What about the
child bride?

We split up, he snarled.

Did you really? I asked slowly and deliberately.

Aye. We did.

What happened? I sniggered.

Doesn't matter, he said.

You know Thin Lizzy's splitting up too? I said,
giving him a way out.

I know, said Spit, turning to the poster of Phil
Lynott which covered the whole back of the door.
They're playing in Dublin next month.

I know, I said. Are you going to go?

Are you?

No ticket, I said.

Well, *would* you go?

What, I sneered, with you and the missus? – no
thanks.

She's fuckin' not going. I told you we split up.

Does she not want to go anyway? I asked.

No, she doesn't fuckin' *want* to go.

Doesn't *want* to go to Thin Lizzy? I asked, all
eyebrows.

I know, said Spit solemnly, fuckin' ridiculous.

Women! I said. Imagine not even wanting to go. That's why we split up.

You were right, I said. Silly bitch.

Aye. Silly bitch, agreed Spit. Can't go out with someone who doesn't like Thin Lizzy.

No way, I said, flickers of guilt making me blink. But anyway, I don't have a ticket.

You could take hers.

Your ex's ticket? I said slowly. You sure now you won't be getting back together again in a fortnight's time?

No fuckin' way! spat Spit. She doesn't like Thin Lizzy. She doesn't like any good bands at all.

Well, that's that then, I said firmly, you're better off out of it.

So will we go then? asked Spit with half a smile. Off to Dublin in the green?

I suppose we could, I said, smiling the other half.

And so we went. To Thin Lizzy's last Irish concert ever. And as we waited for them to tumble on to the stage of the RDS, myself and Spit stood shoulder to shoulder expectantly, full of some strange and desperate pride for our band. We were taking it all in, pointing out roadies and microphones and bouncing with nerves and excitement, when all of a sudden a thick weedy smoke drifted over from the man beside us. Spit looked at me and I looked at Spit and we both stared into the tingling clouds that began to curl around our noses and we guessed immediately what it was.

That's grass, said Spit, with unconvincing authority.

Mary Jane, I said.

Weed, said Spit.

Blow, I fired back.

Ganja, said Spit.

What?

Ganja. It's another word for –

I know, I said, I just didn't hear you right . . .

But we did not *really* know what it was. We had never seen it before, we had never smelled it before, and so this was all a brand-new and very thrilling experience for both of us. But typically, being such a brand-new and thrilling experience, we immediately and very quickly moved away from it. And once we had replanted ourselves at a safe distance, we began to breathe innocent and easy again.

BELFAST

'I don't know if music is strong enough to take us out of the gutter, I just don't know. I followed Dr Martin Luther King because he was the popular one but my sympathies were with Malcolm X. Music was powerful, yes, but *along* with everything else. I believed in taking gun for gun and totin' for totin'! And if I hadn't been a musician I probably would be dead by now.'

Dr Nina Simone

Somewhere in the dark outskirts of Dungannon, County Tyrone, a red light began to circle slowly in the road ahead. Our bus driver groaned inwardly at this unmistakable signal and hushed his bus to yet another unscheduled stop. Time stopped also and as the door pished open, on came a soldier in blackface and full foliage – leafy bits of ash and alder sprouting from his helmeted head. The gun he wielded so awkwardly was almost as big as himself and he had to lean hard backwards just to keep the muzzle of it off the floor of the bus. It made him look ridiculous but not very funny.

And so, gun first, the leafy soldier began to sidle down the aisle, examining the blank columns of faces that gazed back at him like sullen cattle. The procedure was predictable enough – existential questions mostly, like *Where are you coming from?* and

Where are you going to? And the best policy was always just to answer these questions straight. Handy guff was never worth the bother.

We watched as the surreal soldier shrub talked into his radio, pushed a twig away from his ear, and eventually picked on Spit, the only one to have looked him in the eye. Such intimacy was always risky in tight situations like these and it had sucked him into the hole.

Con ah see sam oydinificaytion?

Spit, of course, did not have any identification. He could not possibly have had any identification either. He had no driving licence because he didn't drive and he had no passport because he never went anywhere. In fact, he had nothing which might have proved anything – either who he was or even that he existed in the first place. So he told the soldier no. He had no identification.

So wos yor name then?

Maguire, said Spit quietly.

Magwah, eh? Zammo, eh? Ah's everywan at Grange 'ill *then, Zammo?*

Spit said nothing.

So wheyyou camin' frum then, Zammo?

Enniskillen, Spit said, without moving his lips.

An' wheyyou gahing to then, Zammo?

Belfast, mumbled Spit. It's the Belfast bus.

Dahn't be a facking smartoss, Zammo!

I'm not being smart, said Spit, looking straight ahead, it's written up on the front of the bus.

Ah'll ask you agin, mate. Wheyyou from?

I told you already.

Tell me again, you facking prick.

I held my breath, praying that Spit would not rise any further. But he did. He didn't raise his voice, he didn't lose his cool, he just waited like a loaded gun for the soldier to ask him again.

Wheyyou facking from?

And then, still looking straight ahead, Spit delivered the *coup de grâce* he had rehearsed in his mind many times over.

I'm from *here*, he said firmly. Where are *you* from?

Next thing, the soldier stepped back, raised his rifle level with Spit's eyebrows and began to step backwards towards the door of the bus, all the time clicking his tongue as if squeezing the trigger. Click! Click! Click! Another one, with a moustache and severe acne, joined him on the steps of the bus and they stood together like an entire angry hedgerow, peering down at Spit and talking into each other's ears. They muttered on like this for a few moments more before finally responding to some posh talk on their radio, stepping off the bus and nodding at the driver to go on. We were through. It was over.

Spit was pale and nauseous.

Thought he was going to shoot me, he laughed nervously.

So did I, I said.

He looked like that fella in the Specials, didn't he? What's his name?

Jerry Dammers?

No, the other fella . . . Terry something.

Terry Hall.

That's him. The higher ranking Brits all look like Freddie Mercury but he looked like Terry Hall. Don't you think?

Passing through a checkpoint always brought with it a strange lightening as people flickered back into themselves again. There was always a loose garrulous relaxation that followed the pressure, the anxiety or the embarrassment – a careless outpouring of relief at having passed out of tension and into a different, easy, place.

Usually, it had to do with crossing the border and heading for Donegal or Dublin – going on holidays away from what they called the Troubles and away from the edgy hard North with its complications, its subtleties, its cruelties and its whiny news bulletins.

But this time it was very different. This time we were not passing through some armoured, sand-bagged, barbed-wired, spike-chained, sangared, net-ted, walkie-talkied, loaded roadblock *out* of anything and into somewhere else. In fact, we were actually passing further *into* it – heading upriver like in *Apocalypse Now*, further and further into yet more circling red torches, weaponry and questions in the rain. Belfast, it seemed, really was the stuff of its own depressing television dramas and here we were heading straight for it.

The notion threw me entirely. Why were we on the wrong bus? Why were we going to absolutely the wrong place? Why weren't we going to Paris or New York or Dublin where the streets smelled of pastries, coffee and stout? Phil Lynott was in Dublin. And James Joyce and U2 and Brendan Behan and the Blades and Flann O'Brien and the Radiators and Patrick Kavanagh and the Boomtown Rats. There were gleaming palatial pubs in Dublin and there were gorgeous women with trendy clothes. There were cafés and restaurants where you could have oysters and Guinness and, best of all, people weren't murdering each other in a ritual called tit-for-tat.

My first trip to Dublin had been the longest journey in the world ever. The bus had stopped outside the Customs House and there, for the first time, I saw a ship. It was a huge black-and-ochre Guinness ship and I studied every rivet and rope. I saw a man with a turban on O'Connell Bridge. I saw a Chinese woman and on an island in the middle of the broadest main street in Europe, I looked for the bullet holes in the statue of Daniel O'Connell – shots fired from or at the General Post Office in 1916.

Then we went to the zoo on a big green double-decker bus and I saw the whooping gibbons, the orang-utan with the floppy face and the hippopotamus that wouldn't move. Through the trees I saw the President's big white house and the shady herd of deer, because this was the Phoenix Park – the biggest park in Europe and it rolled out in all directions.

There would be none of that in Belfast – nothing but perverted preachers with bullhorns and rabid women with fag butts and furry slippers. At least if the television was anything to go by.

Further down the M1 motorway and the sky was

suddenly floodlit and glowing. On the left was Long Kesh – now called the Maze – the biggest prison in Europe and the scene of the dirty protests and the hunger strikes of 1981. It had been a very heavy spell in Northern Ireland and not for the first time, the whole place had boiled over and begun to spill.

Following the death of Frank Maguire, the Member of Parliament for Fermanagh and South Tyrone, an IRA prisoner called Bobby Sands was elected in his place. He got over thirty thousand votes and so people half assumed that the prisoners' demands would have to be met and that this deadly situation would be quickly resolved. But that's not the way it happened and the new Member of Parliament became the first of ten to die. It was a long period of television newsflashes and, passing the site of such severe drama, the bus was bound to fall silent into all sorts of divided thinking.

And then, finally, Belfast itself. Milltown Cemetery, the Fall's Road, Andytown, Black Mountain, Divis Flats, the Royal Victoria Hospital, Tate's Avenue, Roden Street, The Village, Donegall Road and Sandy Row. It was all drizzle, street lamps, waste ground, murals, darkness and damp, and my mind lashed itself for its lethargy, for its drift, for its constant aiming low. This should be a Greyhound not an Ulsterbus. This should be New York, Chicago, Memphis or New Orleans and it was anything but. Be careful where you go, our mothers had said, and now here we were tumbling off the bus at the corner of Sandy Row, right in front of the Glasgow Rangers Supporters' Club.

Oh shit, said Spit, this isn't a good start. No Christy Moore fans in there.

Just keep walking, I said, and keep your mouth shut. Just follow everyone else and keep your head down.

Like a Larne Catholic, agreed Spit.

Seriously, Spit, I cautioned under my breath, I'm tellin' you, you've got Fenian written all over you.

And what about *you*? You and your Miraculous Medal? You're still wet from all that holy water your ma threw over you.

Shhhhhh! I hissed as I looked around quickly. For God's sake, Spit, would you ever just shut up!

And so we tagged along with the rest of the ragged band of Ulsterbus refugees and slipped away from the Glasgow Rangers Supporters' Club and out of Sandy Row and on up the University Road with our sports bags and suitcases and bin bags full of sheets, blankets, towels, socks, planted bottles of holy water and the last properly ironed shirts we would ever see. Every man on the street looked like he might shoot you as quick as look at you. Every woman looked more dangerous again.

So what do you make of it so far? I asked Spit when we got as far as the Students' Union.

It's a fuckin' hole, he said. But sure we knew that anyway, didn't we? At least they have gigs . . .

And Van Morrison, I suggested.

And a Kentucky Fried Chicken, added Spit.

Anything else?

Top Shop?

Apart from Top Shop.

Don't think so.

A ROOM OF MY OWN

'When you're a singer you need to sing or you go mad –
that's just the way you are. You feel things very
intensely. You physically have to sing or you get very
depressed. But when you're a teenager it's also the
action. And I wanted the guys.'

Sinéad O'Connor

Spit was hunched over a coffee table, greedily
rubbing together the index finger and thumb of each
hand. There was a misshapen, lumpy roll of paper
spanning the gap between them and I knew immediately what he was doing. And for me it was a real
gunk.

C'mon in, he said, you're just in time.

What are you doing? I asked without meaning to.

Skinning up, he said, delicately licking his cargo
and sighing with satisfaction.

Is that a joint? I asked, again without meaning to.

That, said Spit, waving it under my nose, is a
Camberwell fuckin' Carrot!

I felt like someone had just hacked through my
guy ropes with a hatchet. Everything in this new
place was intimidating enough already – coffee
tables, duvets, curry chips, fried rice, powdered milk
and Kentucky Fried Chicken – but now even Spit

was turning inside out. It was as if I had gone crashing through the looking glass, and everything was arseways. On its head.

Where'd you get that? I asked.

The Holy Land, he said.

Is it grass?

No, it's hash. Red Leb.

Red what?

Do you want some?

No, I'm alright.

It's good gear.

It's what?

Good gear. The blow. It's good gear.

And so I went to my room, put on a Lou Reed tape and wondered about what I could possibly do to tune into this whole new situation. I was so very far out of my element that I was completely disorientated and adrift and it was clearly time to adapt or perish. Here I was in the very red-brick maze of those television reports on the nasal BBC – a place of dimly lit street corners, fluttering tape and body bags – and here was Spit Maguire already on drugs. Yes, this place really was a hole – a bigger hole than the Grand Canyon, a far bigger hole again than even Noon's Hole which, I reminded myself, was the biggest hole in Fermanagh. But I was here for four more years.

Our flat was on the corner of Fitzroy Avenue. Nearby was the Holy Land – a dark warren of biblical streets – Damascus, Jerusalem, Palestine, and so on. The whole area was populated mostly by undergraduates, kerb-crawlers and the few indigenous inhabitants who had tried to live on as if nothing had happened. I was uneasy with the vaguely threatening edge of it but it was now the territory in which we lived and in which we were stuck. It was Belfast and as far from home as anything I could ever imagine – murky, sectarian, dope smoking, Belfast. Bright lights, big city, big nothing.

My Fitzroy bedroom was a dim cave of red and black gloss – furnished with a single bed, a badly scored dressing table, a chair with a ripped seat and a sideboard with all its drawers missing. It was the corner room and so the light came in from two windows on the angle and, at night, a street lamp shone amber around the bed – the shadows of leaves floating around the ceiling and the flaking walls. But mostly it was just a freezing box which promised nothing by way of comfort or relief – its bricked-up mantelpiece and the faded mirror above it always staring back at me like a huge stunned exclamation mark.

But certain attempts definitely had to be made, especially now that Spit had already swum so far into the deep end, and so the guitar was tilted innocently against the wall. There was still no amplifier to plug it into but that had never really mattered – guitars had always been enough in themselves and seldom needed to be actually played to have the desired effect. I knew this well from the Furniture days when we had simply carried them around the town and got looks and comments even from girls with tight jeans and red stilettos.

Then my tiny sliced loaf of books was arranged on the dressing table so as to have the maximum impact should intelligent life ever get to see it – Kerouac's *On the Road* and *The Dharma Bums*, *Middlemarch*, *Dubliners* and *The Treasure of the Sierra Madre* – all school books apart from the first two which I had heard mentioned in a Van Morrison song. I would later go to a second-hand bookshop and buy a smelly assortment of books by the various Brothers – Keats, Wordsworth, Yeats, Blake, etc. – and although I would never read them, they would certainly look the part on the scratched and dusty dressing table.

Then the cassettes were clearly displayed in a neat, properly laid wall – Van Morrison, Tom Waits, Muddy Waters, Elvis Costello, John Coltrane, Bessie Smith, Lou Reed, Dexter Gordon, Miles Davis, the Children of Prague and assorted compilations. Then the precious posters were Blu-Tacked to the walls: Roger Dean's jumping cat, Phil Lynott with his fist in the air, something in Spanish about Nicaraguan coffee, a map of Lough Erne, a knock-kneed Costello, David Bowie as Ziggy and the Undertones in their parkas. And finally I positioned two framed photographs on the mantelpiece – one of Horslips, the other a sort of ex-girlfriend from school. We didn't speak to each other any more but her photograph seemed to imply that I had previously led a regular life and that I was, contrary to appearances, a normal person.

More importantly, however, her smiling, summer-time face reminded me that almost anything was possible. I had learned directly from her that girls could be remarkably generous when it came to the unlikely mates they chose. There was no doubt that if I had been her I would never have gone out with me. It had surely been a matter of sheer, maybe even random, generosity. Yes, girls were not into decent music but that was the pay-off — their generous natures and the beautiful skin in the small of their backs. And surely this huge university, this massive commune, was bound to be full to bursting with tanned, perfumed and extremely generous girls. And, after all, I only wanted one.

This is a lovely room, a tall, sultry English student would say, heading straight for the books and the tapes. I see you like Keats and Wordsworth?

Oh yes. And Joyce! I like him too. He's *very* good.

I know, but is he not very hard?

Not at all . . . once you get into the rhythms of the language you can . . .

And Elvis Costello I see! And John Coltrane! We have so much in common. I'm studying jazz piano in my spare time . . .

Me too, I would say.

And then, gesturing to the framed photograph of my former girlfriend, she would ask sadly, And who is this?

Oh, nobody much. I would say.

Oh, it must be somebody to be in a frame on your bricked-up mantelpiece.

And then I would go all dark and she would recognise that I was more than just a former bass player in a heavy metal band which could never be heard. She would see that I was a sensitive and moody poet who was deep to the point of dangerous. And then she would stretch out beside me on the duvet and talk about Sylvia Plath and her hand would reach for mine and I would swoop. There in my room of amber light and leafshadow I would lean over her and ask: Tell me, you gorgeous sweet thing, do you like Horslips?

And she would be able to name the whole band. Johnny Fean, Charles O'Connor, Jim Lockhart, Barry Devlin and Eamonn Carr. Her favourite record would be 'Happy to Meet and Sorry to Part'. And I would tell her convincing lies about how I used to see them on long summer nights at the Astoria Ballroom in Bundoran. That is how it would happen – all silky and smooth, like expensive chocolate.

Lou Reed was now singing 'Perfect Day' in my damp mouldy room, and as I curled up for the night, fully clothed, under my brand-new duvet, I lay there wondering what sangria was, what it might taste like and why girls never, ever seemed to like good music. It must be their hormones, I told myself, chromosomes maybe. Something like that.

MADAME GEORGE

'I guess songs can be very, very deep – not in terms of meaning, but in terms of experience. More so than painting and in more practical ways than a movie or a book even. The listener can enter into the song and totally leave their bodies for a while. You take a journey through the song and you get to see things that you dream about or that bother you. It can be geographical, sexual, violent – or merely entertaining. It's the idea of the song as almost a living, breathing thing. Ideally, it also has a melody and a rhythm that is carrying you along the way.'

Will Oldham

In the sunken city of Belfast, years before the world went bad, there was a man who might have been a woman. Or maybe it was a woman who might have been a man – nobody knows for sure because this was a very long time ago, and very few survivors of this innocent time can ever be trusted with their memories.

But for the sake of the story let us assume, for now, that this man was a man – dressed to the nines as an incredible woman, but a man even so. They called him Madame George – some say she was a clairvoyant, some say worse but, whatever she was, she wandered the streets followed by gangs of little boys and soldier boys. The boys collected bottle tops and went for cigarettes and matches in the corner shops that creaked under the weight of ancient Belfast merchandise like baps and soda bread, Gallaher's Blues and Gallaher's Greens. The soldier boys drank their wine, maybe Mundy's, and we don't know any more than that.

Across the street, watching this too-tall woman with broad shoulders and big calves, was a small boy who stared in wonder at the strangeness of the parade – the drag queen, the children, the soldier boys; the smell of sixties Shalimar perfume in the feathery dusk, high-heeled shoes clicking and clacking and scraping, ankle-twisting and uncontrollable. And the small boy could feel the loneliness in it all. He could sense, although he didn't know it, that the world about him was about to retch, that the world was on the cusp of something other and that he was caught, before the loneliness set in, in the here and now. In the there and then.

But according to another version of this Belfast story, Madame George was not called Madame George at all. George was Joy and, depending on how you say it, or how you hear it, George certainly becomes Joy with ease. And there is also another song called 'Madame Joy' which tells of a woman going to the university to teach – a smiling woman in fine clothes and shining hair and she is turning heads. Not a man in drag this time but a real woman in all her sunshine beauty, walking though the leaves around Rugby Road, Fitzroy, Botanic, University

Street and University Square, books under her arm, up the steps of the huge white faculty buildings full of mystery and promise – their great rattling doors both open and closed.

But the first version of the story is the better known one. It is a vision of sorts – an *aisling* perhaps – and one of the few genuine Belfast myths. In a city full of guff, rumour, scandal, winks, nods and homespun shite, this is one of the only real legends of the place – the unfinished, half-started story of Madame George. There is something about Fitzroy – the street where I lived and the house where I lived on the corner with Spit Maguire. And my house was the very house in the song and the room where I watched the broken telly was the very room in the song – on the sofa, games of chance, history books, Madame George.

And when the sun shone on the red brick of the corner house of Fitzroy Avenue, this desolate city seemed suddenly possible for anyone still living in it. For once, I was connected up. And taking comfort in a myth I could not understand, I would watch at the window for every man and every woman, older now, watching for Madame George or Madame Joy.

The street, the house, the room where I lived was real for me now and I began to see some reason to be there: the whole thing revealed and rendered greater than it ever was, elevated beyond itself by nothing more than a song. From here on, perhaps other glimpses might be possible because *Astral Weeks*, the album the song came from, had opened up the head, the heart and the soul. And soon, everywhere, I could hear this indescribable music which somehow seemed to have seeped into the very walls of this tuneless, murderous place and was making it liveable again.

GUNK

'Let me put it this way. These songs are not about me.'

Van Morrison

Gunk seemed to be a Belfast word. It meant a sudden disturbing revelation, a wake-up or an unpleasant shock, and now I was getting one on a daily basis. One of the reasons Spit and I had been friends for so long was because we had always moved through our similar existences at exactly the same speed, but now he was making sudden dashes for the line and leaving me stumbling. For years we had both suffered together the same long list of absent experiences, but now Spit was making serious reparation to himself. Not only was Spit Maguire smoking dope, but his latest gesture was more daring again: he was stocking up on condoms with every intention of using them.

Condom was a word I couldn't even say properly. You had to say it posh – *cawndawm* – and I could not help wondering what Spit must have sounded like when he made his purchase. Had he said it under his breath? Where had he bought them? How had he even known what to ask for? What colour? What size? Had he been embarrassed buying them? Or had he been as high as a kite? Had the chemist asked what age he was? Or asked him what he wanted them for? Had anybody seen him? Somebody from home maybe?

How many did you get? I asked.

Bumper pack. Thirty-six. I don't want to have to trip to the chemist every few days, do I?

And he was serious too. He was determined that before the first week of term was out, hands other than his own would be foraging deep inside his brand-new trendy Y-fronts. And he was a quick mover too, because the following night he burst into the house and began leaping around the room in mock slow motion, his arms waving, his fists punching the air and all the time singing aloud the theme music to *Match of the Day*.

What's wrong with you? I sulked.

What do you think? he leered, resuming his theme tune.

I've no idea. Was there a match on somewhere?

Kind of, he giggled.

So what's all this *Match of the Day* stuff in aid of?

I scored! he shouted, leaping up on the sofa and bouncing up into the light bulb. I scored!

You scored? What? More dope?

No, ye bollocks! I got the ride!

Who?

I have no fuckin' idea but I'm down to thirty-three!

So I left him to his musical celebrations and returned to my room to work further, with renewed urgency, on some much needed new identity of my own. Up until now I had been defined only by family, school and home town, and so all of my actions had been duly confined within the parameters of those expectations. And because everybody thought I was a good boy, I had *become* a good boy and this was now putting me under all sorts of unreasonable pressure.

Spit, however, had never been a good boy and seemed to be under no obligation whatsoever, and now he was down to thirty-three. If he kept this up he would be through the whole box in a fortnight and I would still be in my room rearranging my tapes and remembering my generous ex.

Yes, when I joined the heavy metal tribe I had made some weak effort to shake off some of that detrimental goodness. Yes, by playing an unplugged guitar, by being a member of Furniture, Parabola, Rivet and later the Children of Prague, I had taken some steps towards reinvention and a redefinition on my own terms – but now for the first time I had a real opportunity to declare myself properly on nobody's terms but my own. And the place to begin, in more ways than one, was in that crucial bedroom.

And so I stood at the window and looked out at my new home – drunk students, slowing cars, scraggy cats and taxis. It was no Dublin, it was no Paris, it was no New York, and if moving to Belfast was supposed to be have been some momentous move to the big city, to the real world, to the present tense, then it had certainly not worked. But here I was and this was it. This, whether I liked it or not, really was the here and now.

I thought of that Joni Mitchell song about being frightened of the Devil yet drawn to those who are not, but before I had even rewound the tape and made a grand decision, I realised that I was suddenly thinking about Enniskillen – about how much I loved it, how much I missed it with its tarmac and its rushes, its slates and its swallows, its limestone and its pebble-dash. It was almost impossible for me to believe, to convince myself, but I began to feel actually homesick – homesick both for what the place meant and did not mean.

When I was young and foolish at the age of twenty-four
I left Lough Erne's lovely banks, to Boston I sailed o'er,
'Twas there I spied a maiden fair of honour and renown,
'Twas of her I did ask the way to famous New York town.

What would you take young man she said and come away with me?
And we'll talk about old Ireland and Lough Erne some other day.
I have ranches out in Texas, I have acres by the score,
And I'll take you down the Rio Grande that's far from Erne's shore.

How could I leave Lough Erne's banks where my young Molly dwells?
Your poets and your castles, sure to me there's none excels.

Were you ever on Lough Erne's banks when the sun
 was sinking low
With the purple of the heather and the hills a fiery glow?

And the fair of Enniskillen is the finest fair of all,
The lassies are the prettiest and the lads are straight and
 tall.
To Boston now I'll bid adieu for I'll go back no more,
And I'll return to Ireland's isle and lovely Lough Erne's
 shore.

And then the next night when I heard Spit and his latest conquest thundering up the stairs and slamming the bedroom door, I forced myself seriously to work out just how I might take my place in this new exploded world. And as I heard Spit rifle violently in the top drawer of his bedside locker, I realised that what I admired most about him was his total lack of fear. And so I looked deep into the shaving mirror at my spots, my haircut and my stupid shirt, half crying my lamps out, half laughing my head off.

At the first Snack Bar disco I met a history student called Connie. She liked Horslips. She liked Horslips a lot. In fact, she liked Horslips just as much as I liked Horslips and soon it was me who was singing the theme song to *Match of the Day* as I leaped and twirled in slow motion down Fitzroy Avenue – punching the air and sinking to my knees in gratitude like Jarzinhio, the ball still spinning in the back of the net. And then all the next day I sat contentedly on a bench in the Botanic Gardens, my

face turned to the weak sun, inhaling deeply the
thick smell of red intoxicating roses.

ALL BLUES

'That's the beauty that comes from music – if it's enough to express to you, hey this is the true heart here, the true voice. And if it has that truth in it, then somebody out there is going to understand it. It's passing a message to each other and what better message to pass than messages of expressions of love? In a world with the problems that we're having today – my God we need a little love.'

Jimmy Scott

Bart Maguire had completely refused to go to university. He said he didn't want his soul tampered with any further; he had been through enough of that at St Gavin's and from now on he would find his own way as 'a loving angel'. It impressed the rest of us greatly although his father was deeply upset and accused him of being a glue smoker [*sic*].

No son of mine mocks his religion and smokes glue! he said.

I don't.

Don't look at me like I'm stupid! shouted his father.

I'm not.

Do you think I came up the Lough in a bubble or somethin'? asked his father menacingly.

I don't sniff glue, said Bart.

No? Well, I can smell glue in the shed.

But there *is* glue in the shed! yelled Bart. There's a whole bloody tin of it! You bought it yourself to fix the Belleek teapot.

Don't change the subject. And don't swear.

I'm not.

And now you're not going to the university, mister fancy-ideas-man!

It's a waste of time, said Bart calmly.

You should be thankful for the opportunity, said his father.

I am, said Bart.

So why aren't you going?

University is like the catechism . . .

Don't mock your religion, boy!

It only gives answers to questions it raises itself . . .

That's enough of that now!

And even then it gets the answers wrong . . .

God forgive you! No son of mine talks like that and mocks his religion!

It was simple enough therefore. Bart would educate himself. He would go to Tibet. He would shave his head. He would live on poetry and fresh fruit and he would be happy. But of course Bart never got as far as Tibet and three months into my new life at university, he was still hanging around under the dripping bridges of Enniskillen just trying to pass the time. Worse again, because Shay was away too, he had nobody much left to talk to apart from the lollipop man. I often thought about him and often feared the worst.

Shay, of course, was thriving. He had the wit to

go to Dublin and had been in digs there since the start of the summer. He lived in Portobello, swanned about St Stephen's Green and worked very casually for a magazine run by, of all people, Pius 'The Fruit' Mullan. Apparently, Pius hadn't looked back since his mid-match expulsion and was now a star turn in any Dublin nightclub where a bottle of wine would cost you thirty quid.

So Shay was landed. And because RTE radio still played the odd Children of Prague track people still knew who he was. And then when *Hot Press* devoted a full page to him and called him 'The Godfather of Shock Rock', he decided that the time was right to chance it again. He arranged two gigs at the Project and, billing himself as 'Leatherarse – The Man With No Band', he drew a remarkably large crowd on each night. Apparently, they loved him and were appropriately stunned as he squealed his way, solo, through the entire Children/Vomit back catalogue.

The *Irish Times* critic, however, was not impressed, although Shay was quite delighted with the outraged tone of the review. Nothing pleased him more than the word 'offensive' and this particular journalist used it twice in what was a very curt piece. 'An offensive freak show,' the paper said, 'performed by a freak and attended by freaks. Mr Love's gyrations, physical and vocal, were impossible to endure. On my deathbed I will curse the hour of my life wasted at this thoroughly offensive charade.'

Ballocks, said Shay on the phone, it was great!

The place was stuffed and the Prunes were all there trying to put me off but I never sang better. I sold twenty-six T-shirts and there's talk of a record. And there's a chance that the Edge might play guitar on it but I'm not sure he'd get the Fermanagh thing right . . . what do you think?

But Bart had no such glamour or excitement in his life. He was at home staring at the collage of faces on the back of his door and wishing he was somewhere else — sitting in a café with Rickie Lee Jones and making her laugh.

The scaldies and the grebes are good company, he would bluster down the phone, they *know* and I *know*.

And so I phoned him once a week to see how he was getting on, and it was easy to see that there was a gloom descending. His jokes began to lessen. His convictions began to thin and his references began to fall away. It was as if he had suddenly realised that we were his only real pals in the world but that we were gone. We had moved on — nowhere that actually counted — but we *had* moved on. And I could hear in his breathing that his sense of being stuck, of being isolated, was becoming total, and never was it clearer than when I attempted to reminisce with any affection at all about our lost days in the teenage void.

Ah, Brother Declan, he would say, you are forgetting realities. Grass is greener than the rose of the tinted shades. You have them beer goggles on you now, and you see some Shangri-La, some

Utopia and some Xanadu with the Electric Light Orchestra back in your cosy home – but you are wrong Ms Newton-John. Don't forget what it really was – the monsoons, the raffles, the gentlemen's outfitters, the showbands, the discos, the coalman's leathery back, New Year's Eve in out of the rain in the doorway of Corrigan's shoe shop . . .

It wasn't that bad, I would offer.

No, it was much, much worse, he would answer gravely.

So why are you still there? I would ask, encouraging some action.

I am locating my soul among the rushes, he would say, communing with the waterfowl and reading the ancient texts. I have been studying the works of Khalil Gibran and John Donne. I went to Devenish on Tuesday and swam at Sandy Bottom. I frightened the tourists. I hijacked a boat. And I'm listening to a lot of Charley Patton. I can't make out a word he is saying but I don't mind. I am a future hen and I am grand where I am.

And even though he didn't mean it, even though he hated where he was and even though he really wanted to be in Tibet, I actually envied him. I missed so much about that world we had created inside that world which had created us. I missed the nonsense. I missed the comforting greyness and the tasty rain on my tongue and I could hardly wait for the first warm electric lights of Christmas at home.

In the meantime, I had to work out some way of living in the gunmetal winter of Fitzroy Avenue and all I could do was dream of some distraction who might hear music the same way that I did – someone who would shiver to each little modulation, whose skin would tingle, as mine would, to the very same notes. She would have the eyes of Debbie Harry and the breasts of Kate Bush, but for now, just about any kind of comforting affirmation would do just fine – Connie perhaps, that girl from the Snack Bar disco. She looked a bit more like Claire Grogan than Debbie Harry but that was OK. We could still listen together to Tom Waits and Rickie Lee Jones in front of the three-bar electric fire. Maybe with our fingers, arms and legs entwined, we might suspend ourselves for hours, deliciously safe, in the double heartbeat of a pretend but present tense.

NOTHING EVER HAPPENS

'I'm afraid that I put the songs first. If I thought the song
was good, I wouldn't mind what I said in it. I think it's a
matter of priorities. I don't know who I wouldn't give
up for a good song.'

Randy Newman

The vicious and cruel mouth of Thatcher was
everywhere. The Überbitch with an umlaut. Students had protested, marched and shouted *Maggie,
Maggie, Maggie! Out, Out, Out!* through bullhorns
and indifference, but pretty soon we were a defeated
and cowed shower – spiritless and dulled. That it was
Northern Ireland made things far more complicated
and disappointing. Students' Union meetings were
grim shouting matches where the Young Unionist,
Tory, Reaganite, Pro-Nuclear, Tweed Jacket, Support the Contras, Friends of Israel, no-sense-of-
humour Christian faction would shout words like
scum at the Marxist, Republican, Homosexual, San-
dinistan, Shinner, Anarchist, Army Surplus, Oxfam
Shop, Vegetarian, feckless Alcoholic brigade across
the room. And then they would shout back. It was
ugly, depressing and tiresome stuff.

Most students tumbled quickly into stereotype but
student politicians were the worst. Born middle-aged

and grim and keen to impress their seniors (and their heroes) in the parties of their choice, they devoted themselves to the most extraordinary notions and motions. It was a sad circus and the rest of us just stared at the dirty carpet and joined the dots in its myriad constellations of cigarette burns. It was clear that nobody was getting anywhere near enough sex and strong liquor.

But the real sadness of it was that everything here was far too grave to ever laugh at. And despite the thick nature of debate as people farted and rifted aloud at each other, the whole thing was always on the treacherous periphery of being far too real. Northern Ireland was, after all, in a hopeless and claustrophobic situation where the narrow view was always the one you heard – roared aloud from bunkers full to capacity with otherwise brainy bigots.

I did my proper student duty even so. While Spit shagged his way through the Faculty of Arts, I drank my Nicaraguan coffee, boycotted South African goods and voted to rename the McMordie Hall the Mandela Hall. But while issues of international politics were always manageable and comprehensible, it was the local stuff that would really turn your stomach as, bit by bit, you began to understand just how freaky, how insane, how dangerously surreal Belfast really was.

Legless desperation was always no more than a stagger away and so we quickly created our unreal places in which to live and make believe – well-sealed worlds of our own where we could all exist regardless of what went on in reality — either on the campus or on the street. These were the vital bubble zones in which we always floated above, through and around, and where friendships were made and pleasure was pursued. They were cross-community places — hung-over and highly sexed.

And soon, free of the facts, and with Belfast ignored, university became an endless flow of timeless nights — cherry-blossom snow, sleepless blackbirds, badgers in the laurel leaves and hordes of galloping drunks falling into the hedges like helpless bags of coal. By day, we ignored both bomb scares and lectures and slept deep-dreamed siestas in rooms without clocks. One day, soon, we would photo-copy the industrious notes of somebody else and one day soon we would maybe think about getting a grip.

And so I got myself an actual girlfriend. Her name was Lucy and although she was studying music she knew nothing whatsoever about the sort of music I cared about. She had never even heard of Charlie Parker and, what's more, it didn't seem to bother her either. It threw me completely but I went along with it and the difficulties it raised.

Up until then I had communicated with university girls almost exclusively through music — the tapes I made for them, the records I bought as presents, the bands I took them to see. But this was different and I had to actually *talk* to her. Sometimes she even talked back and, most of the time, she seemed to be happily devoted to just two things: her high-class music and me – in that order.

In the evenings I would hunker underneath the window of her practice room in the Music Department and listen to her playing Bach's suites over and over again. There with my back against the red brick, I would close my eyes, point my Adam's apple at the street light and breathe it all in.

But she never once knew I was there and even when I cornered her into splitting up with me eight weeks later, I still never let on. It would only have confirmed her bitter parting words – that perhaps I had been far more in love with the cello than I had ever been with her.

AN ENCOUNTER

'People come to you and say that they have had an incredible experience with your music and you accept it gracefully. But the thing that people love is not so much you as their own experience.'

Rickie Lee Jones

I was in a phone box on Botanic Avenue. I was always in a phone box somewhere, working my way through pocketfuls of change and trying to contact someplace else. When I was at St Gavin's I spent half an hour every evening ringing my ex who graciously and patiently talked me through the night's algebra puzzles. I listened to what she said, took notes, made sure I knew what she was talking about and went to school the next morning with the right answer.

But the queue for that phone box was always far worse than the sums. A long silent exposed line-up in the wind and rain trying to read its own myriad intentions. The woman with the fag butt and the tattered purse looking like she planned a long call, the girl with the one coin out to make a quick arrangement, the worried man with the kids about to ring the hospital. And all of us hating each other for stealing each other's time, for taking each other's space, for both delaying and rushing each other as we dealt with matters so vital to us.

I won't be long, everyone said, but still they stacked up their coins on the shelf like slot-machine winnings as the rest of us stood outside and fretted. But then on those occasions when there was nobody else waiting, it meant relaxing into it – businesslike algebra or even dreamy girlfriend smoochtalk when conditions were good. In fact, when there were no queues for the phone it felt like one of the most delicious things in the world.

But the actual phone box itself was a grim place to be. It smelled of smoke and urine. The crust and condensation on the pitted mouthpiece reeked of bad breath, smoke and lipstick, but the need to communicate with the ex was overwhelming – to communicate so openly with both her mathematical brain and her theoretical breasts.

In front of me there was a list of area codes for places like Coleraine, Desertmartin, Dungannon, Strabane and Tandragee, and I read them vaguely as I tugged the tattered phone book – half eaten and sodden like a giant inky sandwich. And as I sorted my change and dealt methodically with my only worries in life, I became intimate with every cracked pane, every scored graffito, every jammed coin. Do the algebra first, then talk into the ex's hot mouth about Thin Lizzy's new record and the next Killyhevlin disco.

The Belfast phone box on Botanic Avenue was a lighter, less meaningful affair. It was presumably vandal-proof but it smelled just the same. More cidery perhaps than the Enniskillen one but it was much of a muchness. I still rang Bart regularly, not about my own problems but about his own – his status, his isolation back home. And on this particular Saturday morning he was putting a very brave face on it.

I may be an umbrella left at the back of the chapel, he said, but I am perfectly alright. I lead an ascetic life. I continue the tradition of abstinent, studious Fermanagh monks from Molaise to the Hare Krishnas. I am beating my lonely but happy drum.

And so we talked in our usual way.

Are you coorting these days, Brother Declan?

Yes and no.

What about the cellist?

That's all off.

Ah, that's a pity. Although she did not seem to like music, did she?

Only Bach.

Oh, to hell with that. You're as well without her. Anybody new?

Well, there's this girl called Julie Flowers – she's English and –

Julie Flowers? You're making that up, Brother Declan. Although I have noticed that just about any word or sound qualifies as a surname in England. Purves, for instance. Or Crump or Crimp or Ding . . .

Summerbee? I offered.

Winterbottom? answered Bart.

Yarwood? I said.

Norman St John Stevas? Reginald Bosanquet?

Bradford and Bingley? Frank Bough?

Enough! So what's this Miss Flowers like?

A big Tom Waits fan so she is.

Well, then, said Brother Bart, go to it. Women who like Tom Waits are as like curlew's teeth. Surely you know that much by now?

Yeah, I know, I agreed, but the only thing is that if I go out with her, and we listen to Tom Waits all the time, what happens when we split up? Then I'll not be able to listen to Tom Waits again and I don't want that.

Well, only if you *really* care about her. And only *if* you split up.

Everybody splits up, I said coldly, that's the way of it.

Oh, what would I know, Brother Declan? said Bart with mock humility. Amn't I a monk? And while we're on the subject, how is non-Brother Spit?

He's going through this place like a physic, I laughed. He's collecting women like he's collecting stamps. A redhead tonight, a blonde tomorrow, the skitter even went out with the cellist two nights after we split up.

Indecent haste, said Bart.

He's a dog, I added.

A misogynist, said Bart.

A what? I asked.

A dog, explained Bart, and he needs to watch himself. You better keep an eye on that Julie

Sunflower, or whatever her name is, or he'll be away with her too. Julie the Flowerpotwoman.

And so our conversation continued to and fro on a phone line that shot south-west to the squelching town of Enniskillen where Bart was alone with his books, his records and his endless thoughts. Around him, the wind hammered and the rain splattered and the houses and the shops all hunched under their shining roofs and into their limestone walls.

All around me, Botanic Avenue heaved with its sad attempts at being Paris – a pavement café, a news-stand, girls smoking menthol fags and art students wearing shades. But it was a sunny day even so and the red brick of Belfast was at its best. The yellow doors, the black doors, the loaded skip on Cromwell Road, the red sports car, the pasty-faced crusties with their raggedy dogs, the studded punk throwbacks, the gloomy poets in their long black coats – all of them unconvincing but making an effort at least.

But then the thunderbolt. As Bart talked on about the perils of Julie Flowerbed and how the enemy of art was the pram in the hall, I suddenly saw a short powerful figure come marching down Botanic Avenue at considerable speed. The man stopped and waited outside the phone box, fumbling for change and examining a little black notebook full of scribbles. I began to hyperventilate. It was Van Morrison. I turned my face away, hunched my shoulder towards the phone for secrecy and whispered as loud as I could.

Bart! Bart! You'll never fucking believe who's standing outside this phone box.

Who? Leatherarse?

No, I'm serious! I hissed, dropping the phone with a clatter.

Is it Willy the Wisp? came Bart's tinny reply from the dangling handset. Is it Willy the Wisp? If it's not Leatherarse it must be Willy the Wisp!

No! No! No! No! I sighed between my teeth as I grabbed the phone. It's bloody well Van Morrison. It's fucking Van! He's standing right here and he wants into the phone box!

Go home and feel your head! jeered Bart. Brother Van is on some mystical mountain in the American West. Sunny California. *Snow in San Anselmo*. He's hardly standing outside a phone box in Sammy City!

I'm telling you! He's standing right here!

What's he wearing? asked Bart calmly.

A brown leather jacket, I said. Why?

Is it a biker jacket? asked Bart.

No, a bomber jacket, I replied.

And what else?

Jeans.

What's he got on his feet?

Boots.

Cowboy boots?

Not really. But they're boots.

What colour are they?

What's with all the questions? It's Van fucking Morrison!

What colour are his boots? persisted Bart.

Grey, I said.

That's him alright, confirmed Bart. Ask him what he wants.

He wants into the phone box! What do you think he wants? And what the hell do I say to Van Morrison?

Tell him *Astral Weeks* saved your life.

I can't say that!

Well, then, tell him he's a Brother.

You're a big help! I said. This is mad, I'm going.

Declan! Declan! shouted Bart. Wait! When you leave the phone box, don't hang up. Don't hang up the phone. Just leave it hanging, OK! Just leave it hanging.

What for? I asked.

Just do it, said Bart firmly. I'll talk to you later, Brother Declan. You have done well.

And so I left the handset swinging and opened the door on Van Morrison, who immediately looked away and stepped aside to let me out.

How ya doing? I said in a quiet and stiff monotone.

Alright, he said warily.

Sorry to have kept you.

Alright, he said again.

Here you go . . . eh . . . Mr Morrison.

OK.

And then I held the door as he sidled past me into the phone box and searched for the handset. I watched him as he found it, picked it up, listened, looked into the earpiece, listened again and then I saw that he was nodding. And then after a few seconds he said something that I couldn't hear and laughed out loud. After that he put his elbow up against the glass and began a very animated conversation punctuated by yet more laughter.

And so I just stood there and watched as Brother Bart and Brother Van had a long talk down the line between Botanic Avenue and our pebble-dashed estate in Enniskillen. I couldn't quite believe what I was watching and the minute Van Morrison stepped out and vanished around a corner, I rushed back into the box and rang Bart, begging him to tell me what they had been talking about.

I'm afraid I cannot divulge that information, he said.

For fuck's sake, Bart, that was Van Morrison! What the fuck did you talk about?

Well, he said, getting all serious, we talked about music and religion and philosophy. But mostly, Brother Declan, we just talked about you.

IN PERFORMANCE

'I was singing for Dr Einstein on his porch and when he went back into the house I was frightened. I thought I had made a mistake and that maybe my German wasn't good enough. So I looked at the choirmaster and he gave me the evil eye. But I kept singing and then Dr Einstein returned with his violin and played an obbligato. It's just an indication of where music takes a person. I have great relish in remembering this. It's not to be treated like an oddity. I am not an elephant man. I am a fortunate man. I'm fortunate to have survived in the company of great devoted people who want music to have purpose. And that is to elevate the human condition.'

Van Dyke Parks

The Ramones were due to play in the Students' Union and Shay Love, the Man With No Band and the Godfather of Shock Rock, decided to kill several birds with the one train ticket. He left Connolly Station with his new blue hair and, four hours and three bomb scares later, he eventually glided into a mizzling Belfast.

Myself and Spit met him at Central Station and walked him up through the Markets, past the miniature ponies, through a tangle of Saracens on the Ormeau Road and up Fitzroy Avenue to our corner flat – Shay all the time talking about how good the Ramones had been in Dublin the night before.

They played the same song twenty-three times, he said. One-two-three-four! Den-ne-ne-ne-ne-ne-ne-ne!

Spit threw himself on the busted sofa and began to skin up on his chest, but Shay insisted that we all go for a walk. He wanted to see our end of Belfast, he wanted a burger, he wanted to see if Van Morrison was out and about, and in any case, Bart would soon be landing on the last stage out of Enniskillen. And so, with Spit well afloat, we headed out, and we wandered down Botanic Avenue in search of anything curious. Shay just kept on talking about the great times he was having in Dublin.

Did I tell you the Virgin Prunes were at the gig? he gushed. And they were freaked. I mean, those guys wear dresses on the stage but they had never seen anything like me. I was talking to Gavin Friday and he said 'Nirvana in Fermanagh' was the best song he had ever heard. Said it reminded him of the Stooges and I gave him a tape . . . you know, that one we made out in the boat?

I've never heard the Virgin Balloons, said Spit. Who the fuck are the Virgin Balloons?

We were the Fermanagh version, I explained.

That's what it said in *Hot Press*, added Shay. They said we were the idiot savant version of the Virgin Prunes.

But we had never heard of the Virgin Prunes, I said, we hadn't even heard of David Bowie.

And he'd never fuckin' heard of you either, sighed Spit.

No, agreed Shay, but that's because we were in Fermanagh. Isn't that the whole point? We were in the bubble.

In the *fuck-ing bubb-le*, said Spit so slowly that we actually stopped walking to wait for him to finish. In the *fuck-ing Fer-man-agh bubb-le*. If *Dav-id Bo-wie* had been from *fuck-ing Fer-man-agh no-body would-ve heard of him ei-ther*.

He'd have been slagged to death, said Shay. And look at The Fruit Mullan. He's doing quare and well for himself now. Runs that magazine and he knows everybody. Knows U2 and all. Do yous mind the time he wore his ma's yellow headscarf from Lourdes?

Eventually, we made the bus station without seeing anything much. No Van Morrison. No nothing apart from the man who does the football results on the television – Ballyclare Comrades nil, Chimney Corner nil. And so we just sat there waiting in the stale smoke and fumes for the Ulsterbus to swing into Glengall Street and deposit its stiff, cramped and desperate passengers.

There it is now, said Shay brightly, Brother Bart on the cosmic express via Dungannon.

Fuck Dungannon! shouted Spit. Of all the holes in the world that must surely be the biggest! Look at the size of that steering wheel. Fuck me, that's a big steering wheel!

What's wrong with him? asked Shay.

He hasn't had sex today, I explained, he's in pain.

Fuck yous! huffed Spit. That's the biggest steering wheel I've ever seen.

When Bart finally came down the steps with his duffel bag and his apple, he was immediately jumpy and conspiratorial, nodding vigorously over his shoulder at the remaining passengers.

Hello, gentlemen, he said nervously from behind the back of his hand. Guess who's on the bus?

It's not Van Morrison, is it?

Shhhh! hissed Bart. Look behind me! In the red jacket.

And so the three of us looked, taking cover behind the newly arrived Bart and peering into the confusion.

Do you see him?

Well, fuck a duck! said Spit, choking. If it isn't Seamie Sheridan of the Shite Showband Shamrock Shite . . . here, Sheridan, you wanker!

Silenzio! said Bart, putting his hand over Spit's mouth. I was talking to him on the bus. He's up to buy a new drum machine. His old one doesn't do waltzes any more.

But Spit pushed through the crowd and began waving a Rizla paper under Seamie Sheridan's nose.

Can I have your autograph, please?

Sheridan looked all around and muttered that he didn't have a pen.

Declan! A pen please for Mr Sheridan.

And so we ended up stuck in Belfast, on the day of a Ramones gig, with Seamie Sheridan of the SS.

This was the first time Shay, Bart, Spit and myself had been together for months and as we tried to catch up in the Crown Bar, Seamie Sheridan just sat there beside us in the snug, dribbling, belching, farting and saying ridiculous things in his American/west Ulster accent,

Ah'd say now yiz do hev de quare tahms uv it hee-yur wid ahll de wimmin ahn de gyirls. Aye, ah'll hev anuthur wee drap shoorlee. Yessuree ah'm lukin' a drummin'yoke. She'd hev tee bee a gud wan now! No oul shite!

Shay said that the five of us were like an installation in the Douglas Hyde – whatever that meant – and so we all just sat there and got plastered. We told Seamie Sheridan how he had ruined our teens with his embarrassing music and what we would like to do with his waltz-time drum machine and inevitably Spit tried to choke him when he started banging on about the Beatles being shite. But it was good craic even so and so we bought more drink and decided that the only thing for it was to take the SS man to see the Ramones. It would be a kind of punishment concert.

By this stage Seamie Sheridan was far too drunk to argue and having vouched for him with the dicky-bowed bouncers we slipped him into the Union and out on to the sticky floor of sweat and spilled drink.

Ur dees boys gahn tee be playin' up loud? Ur dey rack or what? Ah cahn't abide rack! Ah cahn nivir mak aht de woards! Whad de the bee sangin abaht adall?

Relax, Seamie baby, giggled Spit, it'll harden you!

Uhn who ah ahl dese punters? Uhr dey ahal stew-dints

or sumtin? Ahl ahn dir-ugs probly! Yons de wan way ye cyan listen to thon rack. Ye do need tee bee ahn dir-ugs or sumtin. Wid ye ged a bid tee ate heyur – a bidda chacken mibee?

But then the lights suddenly dropped and there was a huge rumbling cheer as out of the darkness a few coloured lights reached out from the stage. Shay began shouting Gabba Gabba Hey! and we heard a snare drum, half a guitar chord, and two thuds on the bass before the thoroughly startling Ramones walked out through the wash of smoke and white light. Immediately we were right back at that Pistols gig we had never been at, and with the first *one-two-three-four!* we went completely doolally – pogo, pogo, pogo so high – Spit, Shay, Bart and me – thrashing skywards like a wounded hydra.

Sheridan, of course, had seen enough already and had bolted for cover under the stage where he had hunkered unsteadily to sip from his offy bottle of vodka. He was gazing all around him, out of it, blinking wildly and covering his ears. He drank some more and then we watched as he sat down, lay down, rolled over, curled up, thumped the floor and finally puked and passed out. Just inches above him, the giant Joey Ramone lurched over a microphone and sang 'Sheena is a Punk Rocker' (or something very like it) twenty-three times in a row.

KEEP IT COUNTRY

'Ooh, that's just blarney!'

Emmylou Harris

Over those final weeks of the first term our conversations began to change. They changed as the music was changing, now that songs of sheer energy and mood were no longer quite enough. Our lives were changing too, and simply clinging to either comforting innocence or aggravating guilt was becoming less and less useful. We were in real situations now – with real people, with real feelings, and the music had to match.

It was no longer enough just to listen to 'The Boys are Back in Town' and posture in the fantasy it provided. It had suited a time when we never actually had to face up in any way seriously to love, longing, rage, despair, passion, hurt and betrayal – all the emotions that we were now either dumping on others or that were being dumped on us. Now we needed a new musical accompaniment to see us through such brutal scenes both good and bad. It was music which had to be heavier than heavy and far more striking than sheer attitude and pose. Costello and Cohen weighed in and became our cool, wise friends and slowly Spit and myself, in small ways, began to act our age.

Do you ever get embarrassed? Spit asked one empty Friday afternoon.

About what? I asked.

About when we were teenagers and we knew fuck all?

Of course I do. We were a right pair of pricks.

But sure, we didn't know any better.

And we couldn't have known any better.

Pricks.

We sure were, I laughed. And what about now? Are we still a right pair of pricks?

Well, at least I have *some* clue! protested Spit suddenly angry.

Well, I don't know, Spit. I think you're a bit of misogynist.

What's that?

A dog. You've hurt a lot of people's feelings so you have.

And do you think I haven't been hurt too?

I'm sure you have, but you must admit you're a bit of a dog.

Aye, but I'm a wounded dog. This is my blue period.

What's that?

Picasso.

Ah, he's great. I like him. Genius so he was.

Fuck off! There were two Picasso prints hanging up at St Gavin's and you always said they were shite.

Sure, what did I know about Picasso? Anyway,

you're a dog. Whoever blew you out, you can't just take it out on every woman in Belfast.

And what would you know about it anyway?

Well, I know more than I did this time last year, that's for sure.

So what's the answer then? I mean, for all this women stuff?

I said nothing for a long time and then, finally, I dived off the sheer cliff of information into the deep waters of revelation. I decided to come out.

Country music, I said coldly.

Spit's eyes widened and his jaw dropped.

Country music, I repeated slightly more chirpily.

Country music! Country and western! screeched Spit incredulously. Are you listening to *country* music! You're not! Go on! You are not!

Well, at least there are lyrics! George Jones is great . . . and Merle Haggard and . . .

Fuck off! I don't believe you. When did all this start?

Well, I'd rather take comfort in a good country record than do what you're doing. Acting like a dog and . . .

Country music? You're pullin' my leg! This is a wind-up . . .

Well, Elvis Costello likes it . . .

I don't give a damn! It's country and fuckin' western! C'mon, there's no excuse for that. Have you lost your mind altogether? It must have been that fuckin' cello player with the bandy fuckin' legs!

And then we fell into another long silence filled

only with awkward gulps of still orange and Spit spitting slyly around his feet. He wore an expression of disbelief, pain and disgust, but I was somehow slightly euphoric at my confession – a little thrilled at my openness, my maturity and my sudden willingness to engage with love, life and bitterness. It reminded me of the time I left the Scouts.

A half-hour passed with both of us looking in opposite directions. I was thinking about the undeniable facts that I had once owned *Twelve Gold Bars* by Status Quo, *Out of the Blue* by ELO and some live album by Ted Nugent, and he was probably thinking of his own musical sins – *Bat Out of Hell*, something by Journey and, worse again, Foreigner and Styx. And I was just about to challenge him on a picture of the Nolans he once had on his wall when he suddenly started chuckling to himself.

What is it? I asked.

Nothing, he said.

Go on, tell me. What are you laughing at?

Well, said Spit, a huge smile breaking across his tired face, do you remember the time we were down by the lough and instead of skimming stones we decided to skim my sister's record collection? All those awful singles – coloured vinyl and all?

They skimmed really well too, I said.

It was a calm day, said Spit.

Yeah, and do you remember when the water hen appeared out of nowhere and you hit it full whack?

Do you think I killed it? asked Spit with real concern on his face.

You probably cut it in half, I said with little tact, it was only a wee one too.

You know that was an Elvis Presley record? The one that hit the water hen . . .?

Poor oul bird, I sighed.

We shouldn't have done that you know, said Spit gingerly, I kind of like Elvis . . .

Since when? I asked in high-pitched surprise.

I always did, said Spit gravely, the early stuff – the first couple of records and 'Suspicious Minds'.

Well, I sighed happily, I never knew you liked Elvis.

He's the King, Spit replied with great solemnity, for fucksake.

And with that we moved, easy and slow, into some new and mature place – somewhere where two friends, even teenage boys, could tell the truth for once. A place where we might possibly be open about everything, even about the two most important things of all – music and love (in that order). And so, grateful for the freedom, I confessed some more.

Spit, I said, I think I'm in love.

You? Like *really* in love? said Spit from under his eyebrows. Like *seriously* in love?

Yes, *seriously* in love.

Spit gulped his still orange, stared at me hard and wiped his mouth on his sleeve.

Who is she? said Spit, looking furtively around the room for clues. Who's the lucky lady? C'mon, spill the beans.

I swallowed hard, scanned the ceiling and finally blurted it out.

Emmylou Harris, I said. I'm in love with Emmylou Harris.

Spit looked at me with his face all twisted. He examined each of my eyes one at a time and began inhaling heavily through his nose.

What kind of a name is that? he asked suspiciously. Emmy-*what*?

Emmylou, I said gently. Emmylou Harris.

Spit just peered at me, rifted and scratched the side of his head.

So where's she from? he asked cautiously.

Well, I said, she's not from the town if that's what you're thinking.

Is she a first-year? grinned Spit.

A bit older, I said.

You're some fuckin' dark horse, Deccy! Spit leered, suddenly lit up. What does she do? Is she like a second-year or something?

No, she's not a student at all.

Oh, you jammy bastard! he squealed. She's a nurse! She is, isn't she? A nurse! I'll put money on it.

I'll introduce you to her later, I said. As long as you behave. I'm dead serious here. I don't want to see any saliva flying.

Spit inhaled self-righteously and, like a man stubbing out his last-ever cigarette, spat powerfully on the floor with the full unconvincing drama of finality.

There you are, he said, that's my last one ever. Scout's fuckin' honour.

And so, well pleased with ourselves, we settled back and gazed long and hard into the middle distance. That was quite far enough for now.